Puffin Books

Danny Fox Meets a Stranger

After Danny Fox helped the fisherman to win his princess (in another Puffin book, *Danny Fox*) he came home to his wife, Mrs Doxie Fox, and his three children, Lick, Chew and Swallow, with bags and bags of food. They all had the biggest feast they had eaten in their lives, and there was still so much left over that Danny didn't have to go out hunting again for a very long time. But of course they finished the food in the end.

Danny's three children grew bigger and bigger and wanted more and more to eat, and their nice cosy den was getting too small.

Then a stranger appeared on the mountain. He was long and lanky, grey and shaggy, with a prowling slouchy walk. He had lost his way home. Now he threatened to steal Danny's hunting grounds and sleep in his den. He was a wolf.

But Danny was very clever, almost as clever as his hero Reynard the Long-ago Fox. Even though the wolf was three times as big as he was (and Swallow wasn't any use at all) he managed to save his home and family.

David Thomson was born in Quetta in 1914. As a boy he spent most of his time helping on a farm. He did a milk-round every morning with a pony and cart in the old part of Nairn, where the fishermen live. After Oxford he took a job in a remote part of Ireland and stayed almost ten years. As a BBC producer, he made many folklore programmes. He has also done documentary work for the BBC in Lappland and for UNESCO in Liberia and Turkey.

Other books by David Thomson

DANNY FOX
DANNY FOX AT THE PALACE

Illustrated by Gunvor Edwards

Danny Fox Meets a Stranger

David Thomson

Puffin Books

PUFFIN BOOKS

Published by the Penguin Group
Penguin Books Ltd, 27 Wrights Lane, London W8 5TZ, England
Viking Penguin, a division of Penguin Books USA Inc.
375 Hudson Street, New York, New York 10014, USA
Penguin Books Australia Ltd, Ringwood, Victoria, Australia
Penguin Books Canada Ltd, 2801 John Street, Markham, Ontario, Canada L3R 1B4
Penguin Books (NZ) Ltd, 182–190 Wairau Road, Auckland 10, New Zealand

Penguin Books Ltd, Registered Offices: Harmondsworth, Middlesex, England

First published 1968
20 19 18 17 16 15 14

Printed in England by Clays Ltd, St Ives plc

To Timothy, Luke and Benjamin

Contents

1. Danny Fox Meets a Stranger

One day in January, Danny Fox sat on the beach looking up at the mountain where he lived. He could not see his den because it had a secret entrance. It was near the top of the mountain hidden by a hawthorn bush which grew, hanging down like a prickly curtain, from a crevice in a large grey rock. Inside the rock, underneath the hawthorn, there was a small cave with an earthy floor, warm, dry and cosy. This was the secret den where Danny Fox lived with Mrs Doxie Fox and their three children whose names were Lick, Chew and Swallow. Here they would all lie together in the dark, looking down towards the sea through the gaps between the hawthorn twigs, and they would always feel safe because they could watch what went on outside without being seen.

Danny Fox had sat down on the beach because he wanted to think. He was looking up the mountain-side at the rock and the hawthorn bush because he was thinking about his den. He was wondering whether he could make it wider. Lick, Chew and Swallow grew bigger every day, and now there was only just enough room for the whole family to lie down together. If one of them turned in his sleep, the others would all have to move.

Danny yawned when he thought about sleep. He stood up and stretched himself, scratching up the sand with his hind legs and digging his front paws into it, and as he yawned he made a yowling sound which was carried by the wind all the way up the side of the mountain to his den. The little foxes heard it and looked out. They yelped a reply, but Danny could not hear them because the wind, coming from the sea behind him, blew the sound of their voices away from him.

But there was a stranger walking on the mountain who heard the yowling yawn of Danny Fox and the yelping of Lick, Chew and Swallow. He was long and lanky, grey and shaggy, and three times as large as Danny Fox. He was strong and fierce and a good runner. But he had wandered into a strange country, a long way from home. He did not know what kind of animal it was that made these sounds, and he stood still to listen. He was a bit afraid.

Danny Fox's mouth closed with a snap in the middle of the yawn. He had caught sight of this strange animal which was standing on the mountainside only a few yards above the entrance to his den. At first he thought it was a shepherd's dog. But he knew all the dogs in the neighbourhood and had never seen one as big as this. Then, when it began to move again, he knew by its prowling, slouchy, secret way of walking that it was a wolf.

Danny Fox watched the wolf loping down the mountainside. The wolf came nearer and nearer to the hawthorn bush which hid the entrance to the fox's den and then the wind blew a large white cloud against the mountain and everything was hidden in the mist. Danny Fox left the beach and ran up the mountain. He was afraid that the wolf would find the den and hurt the little foxes and chase Mrs Doxie Fox away.

The wind was cold and the mist was wet, but Danny Fox ran up the mountain path so quickly that he felt hot. He ran with his mouth open, panting, and his long pink tongue hung out between white teeth. The mist was thick. He could not see clearly. As he came nearer to his den, every rock and every bush seemed to him like a wolf. He stopped to growl at the rocks and bushes and then ran on again, until suddenly – THUD! – he bumped into something warm and furry. This gave him a terrible fright and, without stopping to see who it was, he began to growl and snap.

'It's me! It's me!' yelped Mrs Doxie Fox. 'Don't bite me. I've just seen a wolf.'

'Has he found our den?' said Danny Fox.

'No, no, but he spoke to the children,' said Mrs Doxie Fox.

'Aren't they at home?' said Danny.

'We all came out to lure him away,' said Mrs Doxie Fox. 'I've got some nice bones and scraps of meat at home for supper and I don't want him to get them.'

Danny Fox stood still with his nose pointing to the ground and howled.

'Why are you howling?' said Mrs Doxie Fox.

'I'm calling him,' said Danny.

'Well, he isn't underneath the ground,' said Mrs Doxie Fox.

'When I howl at the ground my voice bounces up and is louder,' said Danny. 'You call him!'

Mrs Doxie Fox began to howl and, without thinking about it, she pointed her nose to the ground.

'There you are,' said Danny Fox. 'That's the way you always go when you're howling.'

He went on howling with her.

Then one after another the three young foxes came out of the fog.

'Whatever is the matter?' said Lick.

'We are calling the wolf away from our den,' said Danny, and Lick began to howl.

Then Chew heard the noise and came running out of the fog.

'Whatever is the matter?' said Chew.

'We are calling the wolf away from our den!' said Danny, and Chew began to howl.

When Swallow arrived and saw his two brothers and his mother and father on the mountain path, howling, with their noses pointing to the ground, he said, 'Ssh! Be careful! The wolf will hear you!'

And at that moment, the wolf appeared, like a dark shape without edges in the mist, his coarse hair, black and grey, standing horribly on end about his neck, stiffly along the ridge of his skinny back like bristles, and drooping shaggily from his tail. His hair stood on end because he was angry. He was angry

because he was afraid. He was afraid because the mist made the foxes look larger than they really were. Fear made him remember how all other animals believed that he was too fierce and cruel to feel afraid. All animals thought that. So he was angry at feeling afraid.

Danny Fox looked at his eyes, which glowed red for a moment and changed to glistening black.

Danny Fox stood up growling and advanced step by step towards the wolf, hoping to give his family time to run away. He did not feel afraid. He was always courageous when danger came near and within three seconds his snarling lips and white teeth were only three inches away from the wolf's snarling lips. The wolf was growling too. His white teeth were larger than Danny's, but Danny was not afraid. He thought the wolf's face looked stupid and he knew he was the cleverest of all the animals in the world.

Danny Fox stood still three inches away from the wolf's nose and when he saw that the wolf did not move towards him, he stopped snarling and wagged his tail slightly, pretending to be pleased to meet a stranger. He was clever enough to be polite.

'Good evening, Mr Wolf,' he said politely. 'I dare say you are hungry and cold.'

The wolf growled fiercely and moved an inch nearer.

'I'm sorry, if what I said offended you, Mr Wolf,' said Danny Fox, quietly stepping back one inch. As he looked at the wolf's large pointed teeth, he was determined to remain three inches away.

'We seldom meet strangers on the mountain path,' he said, 'You have come a long way and I am sure you must be hungry.'

The wolf growled again, a little more fiercely, and again he moved forward an inch.

Danny Fox stopped wagging his tail, and moved back.

'I was just going to take my family down to the beach for supper,' he said. 'I thought you might like to share our supper.'

At last the wolf spoke. 'What kind of supper can you get on the beach?' he said crossly. 'In the middle of winter on a cold beach!'

Danny Fox could not think of an answer quickly. He was watching the wolf's grey lips, which were curled up nastily showing red gums and gleaming teeth. But Lick, Chew and Swallow came up from behind to help him.

Lick said 'There's a fisherman's house on the beach and the fisherman loves our Daddy.'

'No one loves foxes,' said the wolf.

'The fisherman's wife gives us fish,' said Chew.

'I don't believe that,' said the wolf; but as he heard the little foxes talking he became less fierce.

'So does the fisherman sometimes,' said Swallow, 'but only very small ones. Not big enough for you.'

'Swallow, be quiet,' said his mother, Mrs Doxie Fox. 'Everything gets in a muddle when you join in.'

'Well, they are small, aren't they?' said Swallow. 'And very often there's none.'

Danny wagged his tail again. He forced himself to wag it, though he did not feel pleased.

'Would you like to come with us and try?' he said to the wolf. He wanted to lead him as far from their den as he could.

'First,' said the wolf, 'I must find a warm place to spend the night in.'

'Haven't you got a den?' said Lick.

'Don't be silly,' said Chew. 'There wouldn't be a big enough den on the mountain.'

'He could just fit into ours,' said Swallow, 'Don't you think?'

'Be quiet,' said his mother, Mrs Doxie Fox, but Swallow, who was the youngest of her children, could never stop trying to help; and usually he helped the wrong way round.

'Well, he'd take up all the space,' said Swallow. 'There'd be no room for us. But he could fit in, if he went there by himself.'

'Where is your den?' said Mr Wolf.

'That's a secret,' said Chew.

'You'll never find it,' said Lick.

'Of course he'll never find it,' Swallow said. 'Who would ever guess that there's a cosy den behind that prickly hawthorn bush.'

'Oh, do be quiet, Swallow,' said Mrs Doxie Fox. But of course it was too late. The wolf stopped snarling and growling.

'I noticed a big hawthorn bush,' said Mr Wolf. 'It hung down like a prickly curtain from a crevice in a large grey rock.'

'That's right,' said Swallow. 'That's it.'

'Come with us to the beach,' said Danny Fox quickly. 'The fisherman turns his boat upside down when he's not using it. You can creep underneath and sleep there.'

He led the way down the winding mountain path, and looking back occasionally from the corner of his eye, he was surprised and glad to see the wolf loping calmly along behind Mrs Doxie Fox and the three young foxes. The mist had risen from the ground and as they reached the beach it disappeared, showing a clear evening sky and a full moon that was coming up on the horizon, like a circle of white cloud.

2. Reynard the Long-ago Fox

When there was nothing to eat, which often happened in the winter, Danny Fox used to say to his children, 'Which would you rather have – a big meal or a good story?' And usually they would answer 'A good story!' – not because they really liked it better than a meal, but because they knew he only asked that question when he had no food to give them. A story was better than nothing, and if it was good it made them forget their hunger.

As they stepped on to the sandy beach, one after another, the wolf coming last, his head down, his tongue hanging out and dripping with saliva because he felt so hungry, Danny Fox looked about for scraps of fish but found none. The fisherman and his wife had gone to the town. Their house was empty, its doors were closed and the shutters were bolted against the windows. The boat lay upside down on two thick logs of wood.

'There's your bedroom,' said Danny to the wolf and the wolf crept under the boat. Then he put his nose out and said, 'What about my supper?'

'Yes,' said Swallow. 'And what about ours?'

'You'll all have to wait,' said Mrs Doxie Fox.

'But Daddy said . . .' said Chew.

'We came all this way!' said Lick.

'No supper! Do you mean there's no supper?' they all said together. Then they all started whining and yelping and howling and Mr Wolf joined in with deep, angry tones.

'Oh, do stop howling and yelping and whining,' said Mrs Doxie Fox. 'Your Daddy wants to speak. Listen will you?'

'I know what he's going to say,' whispered Chew.

'So do I!' said Lick. But after watching their father and mother sit down with their backs to the sea, they sat down too, so that all the foxes were in a circle on the sand. They could not see the wolf any more. He was lying under the boat with his chin on his paws waiting to hear what Danny had to say.

When they had all settled down quietly Danny Fox spoke.

'Tell me children, and you, Mr Wolf,' said Danny. 'Which would you rather have – a big meal or a good story?'

The wolf made no reply, but Chew and Lick said what their Daddy wanted them to say. They both yelped out, 'A good story.'

'All right,' said Danny Fox, and wagged his tail, making ridges and patterns with it in the sand.

'Why can't we have both?' said Swallow, whining.

'Swallow, be quiet,' said Mrs Doxie Fox, and Danny began to tell his story.

'One day long ago,' said Danny, 'very long ago, before your great-great-great-great-great-GREAT GRANDFATHER was born, a certain fox played a trick which showed that foxes are cleverer than any other animal on the land or in the sea. The name of that long-ago fox was Reynard the Fox. It happened when God created the world.

'When God created the world he saw that there were no animals in the sea, so he told the Angel of Death to take a pair of each of the earthly animals and throw them into the sea. The Angel of Death took one bull and one cow, one sow and one boar, one stag and one hind, one wolf and one she-wolf and threw them into the sea. And so with all the animals, except the fox. And when they found themselves in the sea, they learned to swim and learned to stay under water for a long time until, in the end, they felt uncomfortable on land and happy in the sea. But when the Angel of Death had thrown them all into the sea, he remembered that he had not found a fox. He searched everywhere until at last, when he was walking on a flat rock that formed a shallow cliff by the edge of the calm sea, he saw Reynard the Fox looking down at the water, whining and crying as though he was very unhappy.

'"Why are you crying?" said the Angel of Death, and Reynard the Fox answered without looking up.

'"I am crying for my friend whom you have thrown into the sea," said Reynard the Long-ago Fox.

'"But you are the first fox I've found," said the Angel of Death. "I never threw a fox into the sea."

'"Look there!" said Reynard, leaning over the edge of the rock and peering down into the sea. "There's the fox you threw in and now I have no friends left on all the earth." He began to cry again, leaning over the water. And the Angel of Death leaned over him and saw the reflection of a fox's head and chest.

'"Can't you see him?" said Reynard the Fox, and the Angel of Death said "Yes. There certainly is one fox down there in the sea. But I don't remember putting him in."

'"You threw him in, all right," said Reynard. "How else can he have got there?" He did not look up from the water as he spoke. He knew that if he looked up, his reflection would go from the water and the Angel of Death would discover that a trick was being played on him.

'"Well, yes," said the Angel of Death. "I am old and I must admit I am forgetful. But if I threw Mr Fox in, surely I threw Mrs Fox in with him."

'"Oh yes, you did," said Reynard the Long-ago Fox, and began to cry again.

'The Angel of Death bent down and tried to catch him by the scruff of the neck.

'"There is only one fox in the sea," he said. "I'll throw you in to keep him company."

'"Oh no!" said Reynard, jumping away, "That would make two Mr Foxes. Mrs Fox is over there! Come. Look!"

'The Angel of Death was chasing Reynard along

the flat rock. He did not look at the water again and never knew that the reflection had vanished as soon as Reynard jumped away.

'Reynard was too fast for him. When he looked back and saw that the angel was out of breath and had stopped running, he sat down and stared into the water as before. But this time he held his head on one side and put on a lady-like expression, prim and proper.

'"Here she is!" he called out. "I knew I'd be able to find her." And the angel came up behind him, panting and puffing and stared down into the water. "My goodness!" he said. "You are quite right. There's another fox here and it's certainly a lady. Well, thank you, Reynard," he said. "You have saved me a lot of trouble. I'd have been searching all the land for a Mr and Mrs Fox if it hadn't been for you."

'"You are very forgetful," said Reynard looking up at him.

'"Wait a minute," said the Angel, who had been watching the water all this time. "Wait a minute. She's gone!"

'And Reynard remembered his mistake just in time. "She dived to the bottom for a moment," he said. "There she is again, look!"

'He leant over the edge of the rock, putting on his lady-like expression.

'"Ah, yes," said the Angel of Death. "She has come up for air. She looks a bit worried."

'"Your work is done," said Reynard. "Now say you are sorry for threatening to throw me in."

'"I am sorry," said the Angel of Death. "Excuse me. I am old, don't forget."

'"How can you be old," said Reynard, "when the world has just begun?" And before the angel could answer, he ran away.'

When he came to the end of the story, Danny Fox licked his lips to show that the story was as good as a meal. Then he looked towards the upturned boat and called out 'Now, Mr Wolf, we'll say goodnight. Stay under the boat and maybe the fisherman will give you something to eat when he comes home.'

'Oh, I don't think he will,' said Swallow.

'You just stay there, Mr Wolf,' said Danny Fox, 'and think about my story. I chose it specially for you, to show that foxes are the cleverest animals in the world. Goodnight.'

Lick, Chew and Mrs Doxie Fox began to follow Danny up the beach to the path, but Swallow, who was wondering why the wolf said nothing, crept cautiously towards the boat, to see whether he had fallen asleep during the story. It was night-time now, but the moon shone bright and as Swallow moved forward, crouching, step by step, afraid but impelled by curiosity, his tummy touching the sand between

each step, he felt more and more certain that there was no one underneath the upturned boat. At last he reached it and found that the wolf had gone.

Swallow yelped to tell the others. There was no answer. He looked about him and saw that he was alone on the deserted beach, alone with his weird black shadow which the moonlight drew on the sand, and the shadow of the upturned boat which looked like a whale. Swallow ran away from the beach, as fast as he could go, yelping loudly as he bounded up the mountain path. The other foxes turned back when they heard him, and soon he was safely beside them.

'The wolf has gone,' he said, panting and spluttering in his excitement.

'Gone where?' said Danny Fox.

'He didn't even wait till the end of the story,' said Swallow.

'I expect he was too hungry,' said Chew.

'Well, we were hungry and we waited,' said Lick.

Swallow sat down to get his breath back after running and said to Danny Fox 'You'll have to find him and tell the story all over again.'

'No,' said Danny. 'I don't want to find him, and I want to make sure he doesn't find us. Let's leave this path and go home another way.'

They followed Danny Fox round the foot of the mountain and began to climb up it by the bank of a stream on the far side from their den. The little foxes had never been in this steep, narrow valley before, and as they followed their parents they looked fearfully up at the twisted branches of the alder trees and at the thick rowans that bent down over the stream. They looked at the moon between the black twigs and wished they had gone straight home.

Near the top of the mountain the valley grew wider; they left the dark trees behind them and stepped out on to a flattish open space where their feet sank into boggy ground. Here the full moon lit everything up and Swallow saw four other shadows like his own. They walked by the side of the stream making twenty squelching noises at each step, five foxes each with four feet, making four squelches each, in the bog. They walked in single file till they came to a large round pond from which the stream flowed. Here Danny sat down on the peaty wet earth and said, 'Let's have a rest.'

'I'm hungry,' said Chew.

'Let's go home,' said Lick.

'I've got some nice bones and scraps of meat at home,' said Mrs Doxie Fox.

'There's no need to go home,' said Swallow. 'I can see a large cake of cheese floating, there, in the middle of the pond.'

'Where is it?' said Mrs Doxie Fox. But Danny Fox was laughing.

'I see it,' said Chew. He was very excited and put his front paw in the pond.

'It's a whole round cheese like the ones the farmer's wife makes,' said Lick, and went into the water on all four paws so deep that his tummy was wet.

'I'll fetch it!' yelped Swallow and leapt into the pond, and began to swim towards the reflection of the moon.

'Come back, come back!' Mrs Doxie Fox shouted, afraid that he would drown.

'Come back, you silly fox,' said Danny. 'It's not a cheese. It is the moon.

'No, don't come back. Fetch it, whatever it is,' said Chew.

And Lick said gloomily, 'Even the moon might taste good, now we're so hungry.'

Mrs Doxie Fox looked up at the sky. 'The moon is still up there,' she said. 'It can't have fallen into the pond.'

'Its reflection has fallen on the pond,' said Danny Fox. 'Just like the reflection of the long-ago fox in my story.'

By this time Swallow had reached the reflection of the moon and broken it to pieces by disturbing the water. He swam back slowly, disappointed and hungrier than ever. He shook himself when he reached dry land, wetting the others.

'Now let's get home quickly,' said Mrs Doxie Fox. 'Do you know the way from here?' she said to Danny.

Danny Fox said, 'Follow me,' and led them over the top of the mountain, down the winding, rocky path to their den.

They followed him to the entrance of the den, pushing their way through the gap he made in the hawthorn bush, hungrily bumping into each other in their hurry to reach the bones and scraps of meat. But they all stopped suddenly, smelling a nasty smell.

'I've smelt that smell before,' said Chew.

'I smelt it on the beach,' said Lick.

'It's the smell of a wolf,' said Swallow. 'However can he have found his way in here?'

'Swallow, keep quiet,' said Mrs Doxie Fox. 'You know quite well how he found his way.'

By this time Danny Fox had crept so near to the entrance to the den, that the wolf's hair tickled his nose.

'It is the wolf,' he said. 'He's sound asleep in our den. Mr Wolf! Mr Wolf! Wake up, we want to come in!'

The wolf woke up slowly, yawning and blinking his eyes. But he did not move.

He said, 'Thank you for letting me sleep here! It is very comfortable.'

'But where can *we* sleep?' said Chew.

'Push our supper out to us,' said Lick. But Mr Wolf said, 'If you mean those bones and scraps of meat, I've had them, thank you very much.'

Chew and Lick began to howl when they heard this, but Swallow went as near to the wolf as he dared and said 'I told you he could fit in. I told you there'd be no room for us to squeeze in with him. So you see I was right, wasn't I, Mummy?'

Mrs Fox licked his face lovingly. She said, 'Yes, Swallow, you were right. But I don't know how it is that you are always right in the wrong way.'

Swallow sat down with his tail between his legs and howled and cried.

'Don't cry,' said his mother. 'Nobody's cross with you.'

'It's not that,' said Swallow, howling more and more. 'It's because that cheese in the pond went away.'

'I'll get you a real cheese,' Danny Fox said. 'You can all sleep under the whin bushes while I'm away.'

So Lick, Chew and Swallow left their den to the wolf and huddled together underneath a clump of whins a little way away. Danny Fox ran off down the mountain path as fast as he could go.

3. Danny Tricks the Stranger

Near the end of the path, not far from the fisherman's hut, a muddy cart-track led to a farm. Danny Fox often went there at night to see what he could steal. All the farm animals knew him well, and the cock and hens and the geese and the ducks took care to keep out of his way. The farmer's dog usually stayed on guard outside the henhouse. Danny Fox heard him bark and slunk behind a haystack into the yard, past the cowshed, keeping always in the shadows, till he reached the dairy where the butter and cheese was made. The window of the dairy was open. He stood on his hind legs with his paws on the windowsill and smelt the delicious smell of cheese. In the moonlight he could see the big round yellow cheeses shaped like wheels. The farmer's wife had stacked them on a shelf, ready to take to market, and Danny Fox thought to himself, 'There are so many. She'll never miss one.' He was just going to jump on to the windowsill when suddenly – sspltt – a large black furry thing spat at him and scratched his nose with sharp claws.

It was the farm cat. She had been lying just inside the window, half asleep, when she heard his nails on the windowsill and saw his bright eyes and black nose. His nose had a red speck of blood on it now and he was whining with pain and growling with anger at the same time.

'If you make that noise', said the cat, 'the dog will hear you and chase you and the farmer will wake up and shoot you from the bedroom window with his gun.'

'I'm going to jump up and bite you and shake you,' said Danny, but he was whispering now, afraid that the dog might hear him.

'If you don't go away before I count nine,' said the cat, 'I shall squall and miaou until the dog comes. One . . . two . . . three . . .'

'Stop,' whispered Danny. 'I want to make a bargain with you.'

'Four!' said the cat. 'What kind of bargain?'

'If you throw me down one of those round cheeses, I'll make your dearest wish come true.'

'Five!' said the cat. 'First you must guess what my dearest wish is.'

'A bowl of milk,' said Danny.

'Six!' said the cat.

'Cat's meat,' said Danny.

'Seven!' said the cat.

'Cat's meat and cream,' said Danny.

'Eight,' said the cat. 'There is plenty of cream in here. Ni . . .'

'Fish, then,' said Danny. 'A large juicy fish!'

'A large juicy fish is my dearest wish,' said the cat, beginning to purr as she thought of it.

'All right,' whispered Danny. 'I'll get you one. Now throw me down the cheese.'

But the cat said, 'Not till you show me the fish.' She knew that a fox could not catch fish.

'And besides,' she said, 'You'd make such a noise, if you trundled a cheese across the farm yard – a big clumsy creature, like you, with your red hair.'

'What has my red hair got to do with it?' said Danny Fox.

'One . . .' said the cat. 'I've started to count again.'

'No, don't,' said Danny. 'I'll go and get your fish. I'll meet you in the morning underneath the bushes by the side of the muddy farm track. Come there with the cheese as soon as the sun is up.' He ran off down to the beach and sat by the door of the fisherman's hut till morning. The fisherman had gone out to sea in his boat.

Just before daylight, when the moon had set, and the sky was grey with a narrow gold streak of sunrise in the east, the fisherman landed below his hut and dragged his boat up on to the sand. Danny Fox went down to meet him, wagging his tail. The fisherman and his wife were the only people in the world who were kind to Danny Fox. All the others and the farmer and his wife and dog and cat disliked him because of his cunning tricks and because he was a thief when he felt hungry. But whenever the fisherman saw Danny Fox, he remembered how Danny, by a cunning trick, had persuaded the King and Queen to allow him to marry their daughter, the princess. The princess was asleep inside the hut and the fisherman felt tired after being up all night and was longing to lie down beside her. But first he had to unload his boat and pack the fish he had caught into boxes, ready to take to town.

'Hullo,' he said to Danny. 'Here's a small one you can have for breakfast.'

He threw a small whiting to Danny, but Danny would not eat it. He picked it up in his mouth and laid it in the box beside the others. 'Please give me that big one,' he said and pointed with his nose to a fat Dover sole which lay at the bottom of the boat.

'That's my most precious fish,' the fisherman said. 'It costs a lot of money.'

'How much?' said Danny Fox. 'As much as half a round cheese?'

'I don't like cheese,' the fisherman said, 'and I don't care how much it costs. But the only person in town who can afford a Dover sole is the bank manager's wife.'

'I wish I could have it,' said Danny Fox, and told him of his bargain with the cat.

The fisherman said, 'Oh well, if the cheese is for Mrs Doxie Fox and Lick, Chew and Swallow, you may take the Dover sole!'

'Oh, thank you,' said Danny and ran off with the fish in his mouth till he came to the bushes by the side of the muddy farm track. The cat was lying underneath the bushes curled up asleep on a large, round, flat yellow cheese. She was dreaming. She dreamt she was alone in a fishmonger's shop and there were so many fish about her that she could not make up her mind which one to eat first. Then in her dream she smelt the Dover sole which Danny had brought and decided to start with that, and woke up purring. She took the fish and began her breakfast at once in the hiding place under the bushes, while Danny seized the cheese and dragged it up the mountain path.

Danny Fox and Mrs Doxie Fox, and especially

Lick, Chew and Swallow, ate cheese for breakfast till their tummies bulged but, hard as they tried, they could not finish it.

'We'll have to bury the rest,' said Mrs Doxie Fox, 'or the wolf will take it when he wakes up.' So they dug a hole and buried it under the roots of a whin-bush. Danny Fox lay down and fell asleep on the place where the cheese was buried and the little foxes and their mother ran over the mountain, here and there, and stayed out playing all day.

The wolf was happy in the foxes' den. For several days he had had no sleep because he had lost his way home. He lived in a forest, miles away, with his six brothers and sisters and on the day when he met the foxes he had been out hunting. He had chased a deer, a very fast deer that had run for miles and miles, and led him on and on until he reached Danny Fox's mountain, where the mist came down and hid everything, hid the deer and hid the way back to the forest.

When he woke in the middle of the day, he looked out through the hawthorn curtain and saw the white tip of Danny's red tail, sticking out from under the whinbush. He felt like going for a walk, but seeing Danny Fox so near, he decided not to. He knew Danny Fox would keep him out, if once he got back into the den. So Mr Wolf turned round and round to make his bed more comfortable. Then he lay down again and slept until the evening.

When he woke it was night-time again. He saw the moonlight through the hawthorn curtain and smelt a strong smell of cheese. The foxes had dug up their supper and were sitting in a circle eating it.

'What's that you are eating?' said the wolf, but he did not move from the den.

'Cheese,' said Danny Fox with his mouth full, 'the very best kind.'

'It smells good,' said the wolf. 'I am hungry. I've never tasted cheese. Give me some.'

'Come out and get it,' said Danny Fox. But the wolf would not move. Lick, Chew and Swallow nearly choked themselves in their hurry to eat up all the cheese before he changed his mind.

'It's nearly finished,' said Danny Fox. 'You'd better come quickly.' But the wolf was afraid he would lose the den. He would not come out.

When the cheese was almost finished Danny Fox took a tiny piece of it and brought it to the wolf. The wolf snapped it up in his big mouth, but it was so small that it only made him hungrier.

'Bring me more,' said the wolf. 'It's delicious.'

'It's all gone now,' said Danny. And the wolf growled crossly and said, 'Do you mean there's no more cheese in all the world?'

'There is one other piece,' said Danny.

'Where?' said the wolf.

'Where I found that one,' said Danny.

'Where was that?' said the wolf.

'In a pond,' said Danny Fox. 'I'll show you the way if you like.'

'I won't leave this den,' said the wolf. 'Not till tomorrow morning.' But the taste of cheese was still in his mouth and he felt hungrier than ever.

'It will be gone by the morning,' Danny Fox said. 'The farmer's dog will take it.'

The wolf growled with a horrible, deep rumbling growl and pretended to fall asleep again, snoring loudly. He thought to himself 'If they think I am asleep, they will go under the whins again, and I'll creep out and find the pond and be back here with the cheese before they wake.' Danny Fox and Mrs Doxie Fox and Lick and Chew and Swallow sat watching him by the entrance to their den.

'That cheese was delicious,' said Mrs Doxie Fox.

'I wish we had some more,' said Lick.

'Can't we go and get some more?' said Chew.

'Did you really find it in the pond?' said Swallow. 'Because don't you remember, last night when I swam out to get it, it just . . .'

'Swallow, be quiet!' said Mrs Doxie Fox.

'Of course I got it from the pond,' said Danny Fox. 'There were two cheeses floating on the water last night and now there's only one. Shall we go and get it?'

'Well, I'm not coming,' said Swallow. 'You know what happened yesterday.'

Mr Wolf stopped snoring and opened one eye. He looked with the one eye at Swallow and said, 'What happened yesterday? Well?' And luckily Swallow was afraid to answer.

'Well, children, if you really are still hungry,' Danny Fox said, 'I'll take you to the mountain pool and find the other cheese. We'll have a moonlight picnic there, a midnight feast.' He led the way up the mountain path. The others followed, Swallow lagging sulkily behind.

They had only gone a little way, when the wolf stood up and left the den. He was very hungry now and could not bear to think of them eating the last bit of cheese in the world while he lay starving in their den. He bounded past Swallow, past Lick and Chew, and because the path was narrow, he jumped over Mrs Doxie Fox and Danny in one long leap and turned round facing Danny Fox, growling and snarling and showing his big, white teeth in the moonlight. The foxes stopped and waited, not knowing what to do.

'Do you want to share our midnight feast?' said Danny. 'Have you changed your mind?'

'I don't want to share it,' the wolf said crossly. 'I want it all to myself. But you must keep your promise and show me the way. The others must go home.'

Danny Fox sent them home and led the wolf over the top of the mountain to the pond.

'There's the cheese,' said Danny Fox, pointing

with his nose to the reflection of the moon on the water, and before he could say anything else the wolf jumped into the water and swam out to it. He snapped greedily at the reflection and it broke to bits. He was so much bigger than Swallow that he made large waves in the water, and when he reached the bank again, dripping wet and disappointed, the reflection of the moon had altogether disappeared.

'Oh you clumsy, stupid wolf,' said Danny Fox. 'You've made the cheese sink to the bottom.'

The wolf looked dismal. 'How can we get it up again?' he said.

'You'll have to drink the water till the pond is dry,' said Danny. The wolf began to drink and Danny Fox ran home.

4. The Stranger Learns to Fish

The wolf was still drinking in the morning when Lick, Chew and Swallow climbed the mountain and sat down to watch him from a safe distance. They were on top of a rock above the pool.

'Hullo, Mr Wolf,' Lick shouted. 'Haven't you found the cheese?'

'Hullo, Mr Wolf,' Chew shouted. 'The pond is nearly empty. Go on drinking!'

But Swallow shouted, 'Oh you silly wolf, can't you see there's a spring on the far side of the pond that fills it with fresh water much faster than you can drink?'

The wolf stopped drinking and looked up at them. 'What do you mean?' he said.

'Don't tell him,' said Lick. And Chew said, 'I'll bite you if you tell him.'

'All right, I won't,' said Swallow.

'Do you mean to tell me', said the wolf, 'that the pond has got no emptier since I began to drink?'

'Drink faster,' said Lick.

'Drink faster,' said Chew.

'Drink faster,' said Swallow. 'Only if you drink one mouthful more, I warn you, you will burst.'

The wolf sat down and began to hiccup, which made the little foxes laugh, which made the wolf growl angrily between his hiccups, which made the little foxes laugh more. They thought it was safe to laugh at him from the top of their high rock, but they did not know how well a wolf can jump. He suddenly stopped hiccupping and ran towards them and, jumping high in the air, he landed on their rock. He was snarling and growling, ready to punish them with his teeth for making fun of him. Lick and Chew escaped quickly, running down the mountain path, their tails tucked in between their legs with fear. But Swallow was caught. The wolf picked him up by the scruff of the neck and shook him again and again like a piece of rag.

Swallow howled and yelped, and when his brothers heard him they came back. They saw their little brother dangling from the wolf's grey hairy lips. They snapped at the wolf's hind legs and, letting Swallow go, he pounced at them. But when he tried to catch Lick, Chew bit him, and when he tried to catch Chew, Lick bit him, and Swallow was dancing round him all the time yapping, and the wolf was turning round and round snapping the air until he grew giddy and saw a hundred little foxes instead of three; and he was so full of water that he started hiccupping again; and he hiccupped and snapped and hiccupped and snapped and at the third snap he caught Chew, but at the next hiccup he had to let him go; and he hiccupped and snapped and hiccupped and snapped and at the sixth snap he caught Lick, but at the next hiccup he had to let him go; and he hiccupped and snapped and hiccupped and snapped and at the ninth snap he caught Swallow again, and then his hiccups stopped and he began to shake poor Swallow as before.

Danny Fox had been down on the beach all this time collecting some very small fish which the fisherman had been unable to sell, and on the way home he had heard all this yelping and yapping, and growling and snapping, and he came galloping up the mountain with his mouth full of fish to see what was the matter. When Lick and Chew saw him they called, 'Come quickly, or Swallow will soon be dead,' and in a minute Danny Fox jumped on to the rock beside them. But he was too cunning to try to attack the big wolf.

'Stop snapping at Mr Wolf's legs,' he said to Lick and Chew. 'And Swallow, jump out of his mouth at once. You'll choke him.'

'I can't,' said Swallow, squealing.

Danny Fox put four fish down on the rock, but he kept one in his mouth, tucked secretly inside his cheek against his teeth.

'I have brought you your breakfast, Mr Wolf,' he said. The fish were no bigger than sardines, but the wolf was hungry. He dropped Swallow and gulped them down in one mouthful.

'I knew you could jump out of his mouth if you wanted to,' said Danny Fox to Swallow. 'I am sorry, Mr Wolf, to see how rude my children are to you.'

'Have you got toothache?' said the wolf.

'What makes you think that?' said Danny.

'Your mouth is swollen on one side and you are talking in a funny way.'

Danny Fox pushed the secret fish with his tongue a little farther back into his mouth. 'Oh no,' he said, 'It's just a new tooth that's growing. We foxes grow larger and fiercer teeth every winter.'

The wolf looked at him suspiciously and growled. 'Have you any more fish?' he said.

'I'm sorry. No.' said Danny Fox. 'But I'll get you another if you want one.'

'Twenty more,' said the wolf. 'They're too small.'

'Well, they're easy to catch,' said Danny.

The wolf growled again and said, 'Where did you catch them?'

'Down there in the pond where the cheese was,' Danny Fox said.

'But how did you catch them?'

'With my tail. I'll show you,' Danny Fox said.

Danny Fox and the wolf jumped down from the rock and went to the edge of the pond. Lick, Chew and Swallow stayed on the rock to watch. They had never seen their father catch a fish and wanted to learn how it was done. Danny Fox sat down with his back to the pond and looked up at them, letting his tail hang down in the water.

'You sit like this,' he said to the wolf, 'until a fish bites your tail.'

The wolf sat down on the bank to watch. Half

an hour had passed away, then an hour, then an hour and a half.

'It's a trick,' said the wolf. 'The night will soon come. It is a trick to keep me away from your den.'

'Be patient,' said Danny. 'You must wait a long time for the first fish and think of other things – every fisherman knows that. As soon as the first one finds your tail, all the fish in the pond come after him.'

The wolf growled and said, 'What other things are you thinking of?'

'I'm thinking of my beautiful long bushy tail,' said Danny Fox. 'It feels as if a hundred fish are swimming round it, brushing against it. We must wait till one of them bites.'

They waited till the evening and nothing happened. The wolf became cross and bored. He closed his eyes for a moment and suddenly a shower of water fell on him and made him open them again. He saw Danny Fox jumping high above him and water flying everywhere from his bushy tail. A little fish seemed to fall from the sky. Then Danny Fox landed, pouncing on it. Danny had let the fish fall from his mouth as he jumped. It had been in his mouth all day, but of course the wolf did not know that.

'Did you see how I caught him?' said Danny.

'My eyes were shut,' said the wolf, and Danny pretended to be cross with him.

'I told you to watch me,' he said. 'You waited all

that time and when the proper moment came you shut your eyes!'

'I was tired,' said the wolf. 'I didn't sleep last night.'

'Why not?' said Danny and the wolf said, 'I was busy drinking water.'

'You're not much of a drinker,' Danny Fox said. 'The pond's as full as ever. Let's hope you make a better fisherman.'

'I am hungry,' said the wolf. 'And it's getting very cold. Show me once more how it's done.'

It was nearly dark. A thin coating of ice had begun to form on the boggy puddles near the pond.

'I haven't time to show you any more,' said Danny Fox. 'But now I've caught the first fish the others are all waiting for a tail to bite.'

'But why did you jump so high in the air?' said the wolf.

'Oh, you must jump high,' said Danny Fox, 'or the fish will pull some hairs out of your tail and swim away. You must jump the moment you feel the fish bite, and fling him out of the water. Besides, if you are slow he will hurt your tail. Come and sit here where I sat and let your tail hang down into the water.'

Danny Fox gave the wolf the fish he had pretended to catch and made him sit down with his back to the pond, his tail in the water.

'Now I'll leave you here,' he said.

'The fish are too small,' said the wolf. 'It's not worth it.'

'You can catch much bigger ones with your long tail,' said Danny Fox, 'and anyway you'll get at least a hundred now I've given you a start.'

The wolf said 'Oh! I can feel a prickly feeling on my tail. Is it a fish?'

Danny Fox went to look, and saw that ice had begun to form near the edge of the pond, round the top of the wolf's tail.

He said to the wolf, 'Keep quite still. There are ninety-nine fish swimming round your tail and brushing against it. Don't move until you feel a sharp tug. Then jump as high as you can.'

The wolf said 'All right. But I'll only stay till I've caught twenty. Then I'll come home to the den.'

Danny called the little foxes and started for home,

but they had not gone far before Lick looked behind him.

'Where's Swallow?' said Lick.

'Where's Swallow?' said Chew.

'Well, where *is* Swallow?' Danny Fox said, and they began to bark and howl, hoping he would hear them.

'Now let's be quiet,' said Danny Fox. 'I think he is trying to answer us.'

They sat still to listen and, far in the distance, they heard Swallow yelping. He seemed to be calling for help.

'Stupid Swallow,' said Lick. 'I'm afraid the wolf's caught him again.'

'Stupid Swallow,' said Chew. 'He'll never learn.'

But Danny Fox was already running back up the mountain to the pond. Lick and Chew ran after him.

It was dark by the time they reached the pond again, but they could just see the wolf sitting where they had left him, with his tail in the water.

'But where is Swallow?' said Lick.

'Perhaps the wolf has swallowed him,' said Chew. Then they heard him whimpering not far away and they walked round the edge of the pond till at last they found him sitting, like the wolf, with his tail dangling in the water.

'What on earth do you think you are doing?' said Lick.

'I'm fishing,' said Swallow.

'Why didn't you come when Daddy called us?' said Chew.

'I couldn't,' said Swallow. 'My tail has stuck to the water. Look.' He tried to get up but could not move.

'I know what has happened,' Danny Fox said and jumped on the ice which had formed round Swallow's tail, cracking it apart with his paws and biting it to pieces until the little fox was free.

'Oh, thank you, Daddy,' said Swallow and began to jump about, shouting loudly to the wolf.

'Mr Wolf! Mr Wolf!' shouted Swallow, but Lick and Chew caught him and rolled him over on the ground before he could say any more.

They said, 'You are not to speak to Mr Wolf. You are coming straight home with us.'

'All right,' said Swallow and followed them quietly. But when they were all safe and snug in the den, he said, 'Why did you stop me speaking to the wolf? I only wanted to warn him that his tail would stick fast in the ice.'

'You silly fox,' said Danny. 'Don't you see he'd be here if his tail wasn't stuck in the ice, and we would be sleeping outside in the cold on this very frosty night?'

5. The Stranger Gets a Fright

In the morning, when they looked out, the black twigs of the hawthorn bush were covered with white frost. Swallow crept under it and, running alone up the mountain, he climbed on to the rock and looked down at the frozen pond. The wolf was sitting quite still with his tail stuck fast in the ice. Swallow lay down with his chin on his paws, hoping to keep out of sight. This was because he had made up his mind to watch the wolf all day in case the ice began to melt and set him free. He did not like being called 'a silly fox.' He wanted to show his Daddy and his brothers that he was as clever as Reynard the Long-ago Fox and the best way to do that, he thought, was to watch the wolf and run home and warn the family as soon as the thaw began. But, unfortunately, when the sun grew hot about midday he fell asleep.

Swallow had a pleasant dream in the warm sunlight. He dreamt about a huge cheese. At the beginning of the dream he was curled up inside the cheese, and at the end most of the cheese was inside him. He was eating his way out of it, but the more he ate the fatter he grew until, near the end of the dream, he found it difficult to bite a hole in the rind that was large enough to let him through. Then the rind began to crack with a loud noise and as he pushed his head out of the cheese he heard another noise, a deep, rumbling, breathy growl close to his face. The cracking he heard in his dream was really the ice on the pond, which was beginning to fall to pieces in the heat of the sun, and the rumbling was made by the wolf who had escaped and jumped up beside him on the rock. Swallow woke with a yelp and saw the wolf standing over him, arching his grey, shaggy neck. It was too late to escape, too late to run home and warn the others.

The wolf said, 'Why were you watching me?'

'Don't bite me and shake me,' said Swallow.

'You must answer my questions,' said the wolf, 'or I'll bite you and shake you again and again.' And Swallow said, miserably, 'I'll answer if I can.'

'Did Danny Fox send you to watch me?'

'I came by myself,' said Swallow, proudly, thinking the wolf would admire him for being so brave, but the wolf came closer and, baring his teeth, said, 'Why?'

'I'll tell you,' said Swallow. 'But please go back to the pond.'

'Why should I go back to the pond?'

'Because I can't think if I'm looking at your teeth,' said Swallow.

The wolf stopped snarling and closed his mouth, but would not move away. Then he said, 'Think!' rather crossly and closed his mouth again.

Swallow tried to think of a clever answer such as Reynard the Fox might have made, and he tried to imagine some cunning tricks which Danny Fox might have thought of to send the wolf away, but the only thing that came into his mind was the truth. So he said, 'I was going to run home and warn the others as soon as you got free.'

'Were you?' said the wolf in a rage. He grabbed Swallow by the neck and shook him once, then put him down again.

'It isn't fair!' said Swallow. 'You promised not to bite and shake me if I answered your questions.'

'Your answers must be helpful,' said the wolf. 'Where does your father find food?'

'Well mostly he only finds stories,' said Swallow.

'Be careful! I'll shake you.'

'But it's true, isn't it? Like the evening when he asked you to supper on the beach.'

The wolf growled again and Swallow tried to help him.

'Of course, in the summer and autumn we have fruit,' he said.

'FRUIT!' roared the wolf, who hated fruit. He grabbed Swallow by the neck again, and Swallow, not knowing what had made him cross, cried out, 'Wild fruit!' in a pitiful voice. The wolf put him down. 'Your answers must be helpful,' he said again.

'Well, there's blackberries,' said Swallow, beginning to splutter and talk in a terrible hurry, 'and cowberries, cranberries, blaeberries and wild currants. And slugs and grubs and birds' eggs, if we find them, and sometimes honey from a wild bees' nest.'

'No meat?' growled the wolf.

'Not often in the summer time. No, Mr Wolf.'

'Does your father never go hunting?'

'Of course he goes hunting,' said Swallow. 'I forgot to mention that.'

'Then where does he go hunting?'

'If I take you to the best place, will you promise to let me go?'

The wolf promised, and Swallow led him round

the pond and over rocks till they reached a grassy slope on the other side of the mountain.

'This is where the rabbits and hares come out to eat grass and play,' said Swallow.

'I don't see any,' said the wolf.

'The evening is the best time,' Swallow said. 'Go and hide in the bushes till the evening. May I go home now?'

'All right,' said the wolf. 'But if I catch nothing, I'll come to your den and tear you to pieces.'

'Oh you're sure to catch something,' said Swallow. 'It's my Daddy's best hunting ground. But remember if you catch anything, you must bring half of it home to the den for our supper.' And he ran away proudly to tell Danny Fox how he had led the wolf away from the den.

Danny Fox was not at all pleased to hear that the wolf was on his best hunting ground. He scolded Swallow and told him he thought the great clumsy beast would frighten the rabbits and hares away for ever.

'But don't you see, you silly fox,' said Swallow, 'he'd be here in our den if I hadn't taken him away and we'd have to sleep outside in the cold when the frost begins again to-night.'

'Did you call me a silly fox?' said Danny, who could not believe that Swallow had dared say that.

Swallow was going to say, 'Yes. Because you called me silly last night,' but Lick stopped him quickly.

'A chilly fox,' said Lick. 'That's what I thought he said.'

'A chilly fox,' said Chew, who usually copied his elder brother word for word.

'What's for supper?' said Lick.

'What's for supper?' said Chew.

And Swallow said, 'I bet it's only a story. But never mind, because I asked Mr Wolf to bring us our supper.'

'You asked him to come here?' said Danny Fox.

'You told him to come to our den?' said Lick.

'To our DEN!' said Chew, loudly because he was more afraid than the others.

'Oh, yes,' said Swallow. 'He's so big, you see. He'll be able to catch the biggest animal on earth. I asked him to bring half of it, and when he has eaten his half he'll be too fat to get into the den, and we shall have our supper here and he'll have to sit outside.'

'Oh dear!' said Mrs Doxie Fox. 'Oh, Swallow!'

And as she spoke they heard the deep growl of the wolf. He was mumbling and grumbling and rumbling outside the hawthorn bush. Then he came fumbling and stumbling underneath the hawthorn bush. And then he came tumbling and trembling to the entrance of the den. Lick, Chew and Swallow, and Mrs Doxie

Fox drew back to hide in the darkness of their cave and Danny Fox stood at the entrance, ready to fight. But a moment later he saw that the wolf was shaking with fear.

'Mr Wolf,' said Danny Fox. 'What's the matter?'

'Save me! Save me!' said the wolf. He was trembling and shivering and quivering.

'What are you afraid of?' Danny Fox said. 'You are shaking and quaking like a reed in a storm.'

'Save me, save me!' said the wolf. 'I've just escaped from the biggest animal on earth.'

'Well, if you've escaped there's no need to save

you,' Danny Fox said. And Swallow, who had crept up behind him and was peeping out, said, 'I told you he would find the biggest animal.'

'Ah!' said the wolf. 'But if you knew how big he was and heard his deep voice and saw his fiery breath, you would run away faster than I did.'

'Did you find out his name?' said Danny Fox.

'I asked him his name,' said the wolf. 'He had a terrible name. But I've forgotten it now.'

'It sounds like a dragon to me,' said Swallow.

'There are no dragons on the mountain,' Danny Fox said. 'The only large, fierce animal that I've ever seen is the farmer's bull.'

'A bull?' said the wolf. 'What's that?'

'Have you never seen a bull before?' said Swallow cheekily, hiding safely behind Danny Fox.

And the wolf said, 'In the forest where I live we only see wild animals and they are all afraid of me.'

'Try to remember his name,' said Danny Fox.

'I'll try,' said the wolf. 'It was a fierce name, a short, rasping name and his voice shook with rage as he said it.'

'It was only a donkey hee-hawing,' said Swallow.

'A bear!' said Lick from inside the den.

'Yes, a bear,' said Chew, as though he had thought of it himself.

'I hope it wasn't a wild-cat,' said Mrs Doxie Fox.

'Well the wild-cat's voice does shake,' said Danny

Fox. 'When she goes meaow, or when she is half growling – m-r-r-r me-ow-ow.'

'That's nearly it!' said the wolf. 'I've remembered now. He said he was a R-r-ram. He made a terrible rasping sound whenever he spoke.'

'A ram?' said Danny Fox. 'It can't have been a ram.'

'It was,' said the wolf. 'Why not?'

'You can't have been afraid of a ram. What colour was he?'

'He was white,' said the wolf.

'Did he go Ba-aa-a?' said Danny Fox.

'It sounded more like Mr-r-r-ra-aa-a,' said the wolf. 'A Mraa -am. What is a R-r-ram?'

'A ram is a Mr Sheep, that's all you silly wolf,' said Swallow, pushing his nose out under Danny's legs.

'Be quiet,' said Mrs Doxie Fox, and pulled him back by the ear.

'Well, if he's afraid of a sheep,' said Swallow, 'we needn't be afraid of him.'

Danny Fox said, 'What did he do that made you so afraid?'

'He had a black face,' said the wolf. 'As black as boiling tar and two jets of steam came out of his nostrils.'

'That was only his hot breath in the cold air,' said Danny Fox, but the wolf went on without listening.

'He put his black face down near the ground and tried to butt me. On his head he wore two giant corkscrews, ribbed and jagged.'

'Those were only his horns,' said Danny Fox. 'You could easily have dived under him and caught him by the throat.'

'I couldn't do that,' said the wolf, 'because he slashed at me with his front feet, and on his feet he wore sharp prongs, two on each foot like chisels.'

'Those were only his cloven hoofs,' said Danny Fox. 'You could have jumped on top of him.'

'He had thick fuzzy armour on his back,' the wolf said. 'It made me sneeze when he came near. It would have choked me.'

'That was only his wool,' said Danny Fox. 'Well, then you could have chased him, until he was tired and fell down.'

'He was the fastest runner on the mountain,' said the wolf. 'He told me so.'

'Even the fisherman's old dog can run faster than a sheep,' said Swallow, peeping out this time from under his father's chin.

The wolf looked nastily at Swallow and said, 'He'll be here in a minute and then we shall see who runs fastest.'

'Sit down, Mr Wolf, and save your strength,' said Danny Fox. 'You say this ram chased you here?'

The wolf was afraid to sit down. He crouched and

fidgeted, here and there, between the hawthorn and the cave, looking first to one side, then the other, then behind him, and cocking his ears to listen, this way and that, for the terrible sound of galloping cloven hoofs.

'Sit down, Mr Wolf,' said Danny Fox again. 'We've been talking a long time now, haven't we? If the ram was really chasing you, he would be here by now.'

He persuaded the wolf to sit outside the cave and Mrs Doxie Fox and Lick, Chew and Swallow lay down inside and slept, with Danny at the entrance of their den to guard them.

6. Danny Takes the Stranger Hunting

The wolf groaned with fear and hunger all through the night, but when daylight came he felt braver, thinking that the ram would never find him, and as soon as he felt safe he snarled and growled and pushed Danny roughly with his nose.

'Let me into the den!' he said. 'And give me my breakfast.'

'You'll get your breakfast soon,' said Danny, 'but not here.'

'Let me in!' snarled the wolf.

'There's no room!' said Danny, snapping at his feet.

'Then throw my food out!'

'We haven't any food,' said Danny Fox. 'But if you do what I tell you, I promise you a big breakfast.'

'How big?' said the wolf, remembering the small fish and the mouthful of cheese.

'Was the ram as big as you?' said Danny Fox.

'Twice as big!' said the wolf and began to tremble with fear again.

'Then your breakfast will be twice as big as you,' said Danny Fox. 'You can have the ram for breakfast and give us what's left over.'

The wolf was shaking from his nose to his toes. 'I'd rather starve to death,' he said, 'than meet that r-r-r . . what do you call it? . . . than look that ferocious, fiery furnace in the eye again!'

'What do you mean?' said Danny, teasing him.

'That r-r-r-r-rumbling thing with horns. You said its name just now.'

'The ram?' said Danny.

'Don't speak so loud. He might hear!'

'Go back to the place where you found him,' said Danny Fox, 'and catch him and bring him here.'

'You go!' said the wolf.

'I'm not big enough to catch him,' Danny Fox explained. 'But you with your long legs and wide mouth . . . ! Can't you understand that the ram is afraid of *you*?'

The wolf would not believe him. 'It's another of

your tricks,' he said and he refused to go out hunting until Danny promised to go with him.

Then Danny Fox led the way up the mountain path to the big grey rock, and round the edge of the pond and over the small rocks until they could see the grassy slope on the other side of the mountain. Here he walked stealthily with his nose to the ground. 'Is this where you met the ram?' he said. The wolf did not answer and Danny walked on.

'Whereabouts did you meet him?' said Danny, looking this way and that for the ram. The wolf did not answer and Danny walked on. He could see no sheep, no hares, nor even the smallest rabbit. No animals at all had come to eat the grass and play, and this was because they knew the wolf was on the mountain. The hares had gone to lie in the thick heather, holding their long ears up to listen for the footsteps of the wolf, and twitching their delicate nostrils to catch the smell of him in the cold wind. The rabbits were hiding deep in their burrows, huddled together in the dark earth. And the ram had led his flock of sheep into a corner where they were hidden by a thick stone wall. There was one little lamb in the flock, the first lamb to be born that year. It was only seven days old. It was hiding underneath its mother and its mother was hiding behind the big ram. Danny Fox went prowling round the grassy place till he came to the top of a green hillock. From there he looked down and saw the ram on guard with the herd of sheep behind him, against the stone wall. 'Come on, Mr Wolf!' he said, but again there was no answer. He looked round, this time, and saw there was no wolf. The wolf had run back to the rocks. Danny knew he was too small to attack a ram by himself, so he had to turn back and search for him.

When the wolf saw Danny Fox trotting back unharmed, he came out of his hiding place, and went to meet him growling quietly.

He said: 'It is just as I thought, Danny Fox. You dare not go near the ram.'

'Why didn't you come with me?' Danny Fox said.

'Because I knew you'd run away when we got close, and leave me alone to face the ram.'

'Aren't you hungry any more?' said Danny.

'Of course I am, but I don't want my breakfast to eat me.'

'The ram couldn't eat you, you foolish wolf,' said Danny Fox. 'But I'll tell you what I'll do; I'll fetch a rope and tie myself on to you. Then you'll know I can't run away whatever happens. Hide in these rocks while I fetch it.'

The wolf lay down between the rocks and Danny Fox galloped away.

On the beach he found a long piece of rope which the fisherman had thrown away. It was too old and weak to hold the heavy fishing nets, but strong enough to keep a fox and wolf together and Danny Fox dragged it up the mountain and twisted one end round the neck of the wolf and the other round his own neck so firmly that they could not get away from each other however hard they tried. They then set off prowling slowly down the grassy slope towards the place where the ram and his flock of sheep were huddled against a wall. The wolf hung back but Danny pulled him along.

The big ram heard them and smelt them. For a minute he stepped forward to look at them, leaving the ewes and the newborn lamb crouching in the

shelter of the wall. But when he saw the wolf and Danny Fox and the long rope that joined them together, he ran back to the ewes and the lamb and told them, bleating pitifully, that they would all be killed. All the sheep began to baaa and maaa in sorrow and fear, and when the wolf heard them he sat down suddenly, jerking Danny Fox by the neck with the rope.

'We'll have to give it up,' he said. 'Listen to the noise. There's an army of sheep against us and we are only two.'

All the sheep except the mother of the newborn lamb were trembling with fear, but the mother walked up to the ram and said, 'Take my lamb and go up to the top of the grassy slope. My little lamb will cry when you take him from me and you can comfort him when you get near the wolf by shouting "There's your dinner". Look hard at the wolf as you say "There's your dinner!"'

The ram led the little lamb away from the flock towards the place where Danny Fox and the wolf were sitting, and all the way up the hill the lamb was bleating and crying for its mother.

The ram put on his gruffest voice and said 'It's all right, my dear. I know you are hungry.'

This made the lamb bleat more loudly.

'Don't worry, my dear,' said the ram. 'We shall soon catch the wolf.'

This made the lamb bleat more loudly than ever.

'Stop bleating,' said the ram, as they came to the top of the grassy slope. 'I can see a big fat wolf. How delicious!'

When the wolf heard this he called out, 'I'm not fat,' and tried to run away, but Danny dug his paws into the ground and the rope held fast.

'The fattest wolf I've ever seen!' said the ram, coming closer, with the little lamb beside him.

'I'm as thin as a rake,' said the wolf.

'As fat as butter,' said the ram.

'I'm as hard as nails,' said the wolf.

'As soft as mashed potatoes,' said the ram.

'I'm as dry as dust,' said the wolf.

'You're as juicy as a pear,' said the ram coming closer.

The wolf tugged the rope, but Danny would not let him run away.

'Come nearer and feel him,' said Danny who was planning to run round the ram and tangle him up in the rope.

'I can see from here that he's perfect,' said the ram. 'How kind you are, Danny Fox, to bring us a wolf for our dinner.'

'Are you ready to eat him now?' said Danny Fox.

The ram stared at the wolf and spoke in his gruffest voice and said, 'We are ready to eat him now!'

When the wolf heard that he jumped with fright. He jumped backwards and jerked the rope, pulling Danny over. He was more afraid than ever now that he thought Danny was on the ram's side. And he began to run without looking where he was going, dragging Danny Fox along behind him, bumping and sliding and scraping and gliding, uphill and downhill through moorland and bog, over pebbles and rocks, through bushes and heather and thistles and docks, in the sun and the rain and the hail and the sleet and the snow. It was almost night-time when they reached the snowy land. The wind blew snow into their eyes and they could not see. Danny shouted to the wolf to stop, but the wolf would not listen and went galloping on as fast as ever until he fell with Danny after him, helter-skelter, higgledy-piggledy over the edge of a cliff. The cliff was high, but luckily the snow at the bottom was deep and they fell into a soft bed, tangled together with the rope. They were so tired and out of breath that they forgot to be cross with each other. They dug a warm cave in the snow, like an Eskimo's igloo, and went to sleep.

7. Danny Fox's Punishment

When Danny Fox opened his eyes in the morning, he saw that he was in a strange country far away from home. There was a thick forest of pine trees below him, their branches laden with snow, and behind him stood the high rocky cliff down which he had fallen with the wolf. There seemed to be no way of escape from this place and he thought to himself, 'Even if I did escape, I should not know which way to go.' He yawned and stretched his legs, and began to walk through the snow towards the forest, but he had forgotten that he was attached to the wolf, and when the rope stretched tight he heard a terrible snarling and growling behind him. He looked round and saw that he had woken the wolf and tumbled him over in the snow. The wolf turned several somersaults, standing first on his head and next on his tail. He floundered clumsily about till the rope became entangled in all his four legs and he had to lie down and call for help.

Danny Fox went back to look at him.

'Undo the rope, I can't move,' said the wolf.

'Oh-ho,' said Danny Fox. 'At last you are my prisoner.'

'Set me free,' said the wolf. 'Untwist the rope and set my legs free.'

'I will not set you free,' said Danny Fox, 'until you show me my way home.'

'I don't know your way home,' said the wolf. 'But it looks to me as if I am near my own home.' He held up his head and pointed his nose to the sky and howled the longest and most mournful howl that Danny had ever heard. 'Oo-loo-loo-loo!' cried the wolf.

Danny Fox stood still, surprised to hear a call so sad and loud, and in a moment came an answer – 'Oo-loo-loo-loo!' – from far away.

'Was that an echo?' said Danny, barking loudly and holding his head on one side to listen for the echo of his bark.

No echo came. There was no sound except for the croak of a raven who sat watching on a ledge half-way up the cliff.

'Oo-loo-loo-loo,' cried the wolf again and now

there were two answers from different parts of the forest.

Again Danny barked and stopped to listen for the echo of his bark, but no sound came except the alarm note of a blackbird who was whistling to warn his friends that a wolf and a fox were near.

'Oo-loo-loo-loo,' cried the wolf again, and now there were three answers from different parts of the forest.

The wolf howled again and again and again and every time the answering howls came nearer until there was a chorus of six oo-loo-loo-loo's nearby. Danny Fox looked at the wolf. 'What is it?' he said. 'It isn't an echo.'

The wolf wagged his tail.

'Why do you wag your tail, you foolish wolf?' said Danny. 'There you lie in the snow, my prisoner, with your legs tied together. What have you got to be pleased about?'

'My brothers and sisters are coming,' said the wolf. 'All six of them answered when I howled.'

Danny peered into the darkness of the forest, but saw nothing move.

'They are hiding among the trees,' said the wolf.

Danny peered again into the forest and saw grey shapes like hay or withered weeds among the trees.

'Can you see my brothers and sisters?' said the wolf.

'Do your brothers look like wispy hay?' said Danny Fox. 'Do your sisters look like lanky withered weeds?'

'They are all grey with smudges of black, and long hair, if that's what you mean,' said the wolf, and suddenly the grey shapes in the forest began to move.

'I am not afraid,' said Danny Fox, but secretly he wanted to run away and as he spoke he began to gnaw the rope which bound him to the wolf.

The grey shapes in the forest moved slowly on. At first they were blurred like a mist which crept along the ground, but as they emerged from the trees, Danny saw them, one by one, rough angry giants like dogs, with matted hair, red tongues and blood-shot eyes. Danny Fox stopped gnawing the rope and watched them as they formed a semicircle round him and his wolf. They stalked him. Six grey-black noses pointed at him. Six snarling mouths came nearer and nearer, step by step, quite silent on the snow, without a growl, without a breathy sound. But the breath from six mouths looked like steam in the cold air. Six grey tails stood stiffly up. Six tawny necks bristled angrily, with hair on end. And Danny Fox looked from one to the other and behind him at the cliff, and saw no way of escape.

'Dear wolves,' said Danny Fox in his sweetest voice. 'How happy you are to see me.'

But the wolves were not happy at all. They growled six growls in a chorus and came closer. Danny Fox was afraid, but he wagged his tail, pretending to be pleased.

He said, 'Dear wolves, I have brought your brother back to you. He was lost on the mountain.'

The oldest of the six wolves bared his teeth and said, 'Why did you tie my brother up?'

'He was afraid to jump down the cliff,' said Danny Fox. 'I had to tie his legs together and throw him down.'

'That's not true,' said the tied-up wolf and immediately all his brothers and sisters pounced on the rope and gnawed it until they set him free. But the oldest wolf held the end of the rope in his teeth and kept Danny Fox a prisoner.

Now Danny Fox was surrounded by seven angry wolves. The sun shone bright on the snow and he looked about him for a way of escape. He saw a black hole at the root of one of the pine trees and said to himself 'If I could hide there, I'd be safe. It's big enough for me and too small for a wolf.'

Then he wagged his tail again, pretending to be happy, and said, 'I am hungry, and I'm sure your brother wolf whom I've brought home to you is hungry too.'

'Yes, I am!' said the wolf and kicked the last scraps of broken rope away from him.

'Well,' said Danny. 'Can you smell cheese sandwiches, or anything like that?'

All seven wolves began to sniff the air.

The oldest wolf said, 'I don't know what cheese is. But I can smell a good smell and it comes from the edge of the forest.'

Danny Fox's special wolf began to howl with hunger. 'It is cheese,' he said. 'I've tasted cheese in the fox's den. It is delicious.'

All seven wolves turned their backs on Danny at once and walked quietly step by step towards the forest. This was because they didn't know what cheese was. They thought it might run away if it heard their footsteps. They walked towards the tree where the black hole was but, unluckily for Danny, the oldest wolf remembered to keep the end of the rope in his mouth. Danny Fox was still a prisoner.

All seven wolves tried to poke their noses under the root of the tree at the same time. They smelt something delicious there, but the hole between the roots was too small for them and after yelping with delight, they began to snap at each other and quarrel. While they were quarrelling, Danny Fox crept nearer and nearer to the hole and looked in.

And there he saw something that made his mouth water. The hole had been used by the forestry men as a hiding place for their dinner. Danny counted six hard-boiled eggs and twelve sandwiches. By

straining at his rope, he nearly reached them, but the old wolf pulled him back.

'Listen to me,' said Danny Fox to the quarrelling wolves, and barked at them fiercely until they were quiet. 'The forestry men have left their dinner in that hole. There's plenty for all of us. We can have a feast. But you'll have to let me get it out for you.'

'Oh no!' said Danny's special wolf. 'He'll trick us!' And he told his brothers and sisters of all the tricks Danny had played on him while he was away.

'The fox must be punished,' the old wolf said. 'How shall we punish him, brothers and sisters?'

'Let's tear him to pieces,' the second wolf said, and they all began barking and shouting, 'Tear him to pieces! Tear him to pieces!'

'Poor wolves,' said Danny when at last they stopped. 'You can't think of very bad punishments, can you? I have always longed to be torn to pieces by seven wolves and now it looks as if my dream will soon come true!'

The seven wolves stared at him and the oldest one said, 'What do you hate most in all the world?'

'I hate being tied up to trees,' he said and took a step or two towards the place where the food was hidden. But the oldest wolf pulled him back, saying, 'No, not that tree! If we tied you there, you'd eat all the food yourself.' He dragged Danny into the forest and Danny was careful to count the trees they passed as he walked along at the end of the rope. When they reached the seventh tree from the hole where the food was hidden, the old wolf stopped and began to tie him up, but as soon as the others saw this, they snarled and snapped at each other, saying 'It's not fair! I want to punish him! I want to tie him up! It isn't fair!'

'All right,' said the oldest wolf, 'but be quiet. We can't all tie him up, can we? We must think of another punishment. What else do you hate, Danny Fox?'

'I love dancing,' Danny Fox said. 'And I hate being tied up to trees while other animals are happily dancing.'

The oldest wolf said, 'There you are, then. If we all dance together, we shall all have a share in the punishment.'

'All the same, only one can tie him up,' said the youngest wolf, 'and that will still be unfair.'

'Why don't you take it in turns?' said Danny Fox. 'Each of you can tie me to a different tree.'

And the wolves shouted 'Yes' seven times. But Danny's special wolf was suspicious. 'Will you really hate it?' he snarled.

'I'll hate it,' said Danny.

'Good,' said the wolf, and they all came close to him growling.

8. The Dance of the Seven Wolves

When the wolves gathered round him growling, Danny Fox pretended to be afraid.

'Please don't tie me to this tree,' he said.

'Oh, yes, I shall,' said the oldest wolf, and he walked round the tree with the end of the rope in his mouth, made a loop, jumped through it, still holding the rope, and pulled it tightly into a knot.

'That is quite enough punishment,' Danny Fox said. 'Please, please do not dance!'

'Oh, yes, we shall dance!' said the oldest wolf. 'But what kind of dance shall we dance?'

'Try the fox-trot,' said Danny.

'Most certainly not,' said the wolves and they all spoke together, each wolf choosing two or three dances. They were barking and jumping and skipping about in the snow. Danny Fox sat down to listen to them and this is what he heard.

'Let us shake.'

'Let us quake.'

'Let us twist, I insist.'

'No, no, no, let's dance the tango.'

'I prefer a quick fandango.'

'Let us dance the Highland fling.'

'Let us trip it in a ring.'

'Dance the rumba.'

'Dance the samba.'

'Let us whirl.'

'Let us twirl.'

'Let me try to pirouette.'

'We'll dance a stately minuet.'

'I prefer the Square Quadrille.'

'But I prefer an Eightsome Reel.'

'No, no, no, let's Rock and Roll!'

'YOU WOLVES WILL DRIVE ME UP THE POLE!'

The last eight words were spoken by Danny Fox, in a loud and angry voice. The wolves became silent at once and turned to look at him.

Danny Fox said, 'You will never agree on a dance unless you listen to each other. I can see that you are too stupid to listen to each other, so your only hope of choosing a dance is to listen to me. Because I am not stupid. I am the cleverest, handsomest, wisest animal in all the world.'

'Which dance do you love most?' said the oldest wolf. 'Which dance would make you saddest when you found you couldn't join in?'

'The dance I love most is the Dance of the Seven Wolves.'

The seven wolves sat down in the snow and said, 'What's that?'

Danny Fox said, 'How many trees can you count from here to the edge of the forest?' and the seven wolves answered, 'Seven.'

'That is one tree for each of you. At each tree a different wolf will lead the dance.'

'And a different wolf will tie you to each tree!' said the old one, licking his lips.

His red tongue, his grey lips and his white teeth made Danny Fox afraid, but he only said, 'Be quiet for a minute or two, while I try to remember how it goes.'

The truth was that until that moment no one in the world had heard of the Dance of the Seven Wolves. Danny Fox had invented the name and now he had to work out how to dance it. He wanted to trick the wolves into leaving him alone for a few minutes by each tree. He hoped to excite them, to make them enjoy the dance so much, that in the end they would forget to watch him, and tie him to the seventh tree where the food was hidden, and dance away, turning their backs on him. Then he would be able to hide in the hole, which was too small for them to enter.

He said, 'There are seven wolves and seven trees and seven dances. At every tree you must choose a leader and go dancing after him, away from me, until I bark. As soon as you hear me bark, race back. The first one to reach me must undo the knot and lead me to the next tree.'

'Be careful, brothers and sisters,' said Danny's special wolf. 'It may be one of his tricks.'

But the oldest wolf said, 'He cannot trick us if we make the rope secure.' The oldest wolf, being very fond of dancing, was in a hurry to begin. 'I am the first leader,' he said, and stood on his hind legs with his back to the tree.

And so the wolves began to dance away from Danny Fox, leaping and tripping and skipping and turning in circles, some on their hind legs, some on all four legs, yelping and howling with joy. Danny Fox did not let them go far away from him the first time. He barked, and they came racing back.

The second wolf tied him to the next tree and again they went dancing away until they heard him bark. Then the third wolf tied him to the third tree, and the fourth to the next and the fifth to the next, and at each tree he let them go dancing a little bit farther away. Each tree brought him nearer to the hole where the food was hidden. His mouth began to water as he thought of that, shivering in the snow, and the dribbles from his tongue turned to icicles. But the wolves kept themselves warm by dancing.

When they tied him to the sixth tree, he could smell the cheese sandwiches, but the wolves were so excited that they thought of nothing but the dance. He let them dance a long time at the sixth tree, and it was only when he barked and they came racing back that he began to fear that they would smell the cheese. So as soon as they untied him from the sixth tree he pulled the rope out to its full length and ran quickly away.

The wolves came after, holding the end of the long rope, but by the time they reached the seventh tree, where the food was hidden, there was no smell of cheese, nor any hole to be seen because Danny Fox was lying over the hole like a lid.

The seventh wolf now tied him to the seventh tree and said, 'Why are you lying down?'

'I am tired,' said Danny. 'You have punished me too hard.' He began to pant and whimper, saying, 'Please don't dance again!'

'Oh yes, we will,' said the oldest wolf. 'You said there were seven dances. We have only had six.'

The youngest wolf said, 'It is my turn to be leader. Of course we must dance.' And he jumped over Danny Fox and turned in circles, chasing his tail, making the snow fly up from the ground with his big paws.

The wolves were frantic with excitement because they knew it was their last dance. They ran round and round the tree, barking and growling and biting each other's necks in fun, and soon they went away from Danny Fox, dancing, capering, prancing, flouncing, bouncing over the snow. It was Danny's plan to make this the longest dance of all. He needed plenty of time to himself and had decided to let them dance far, far away before he called them back. As for the wolves, they forgot all about him, and while they were frisking and frolicking, gambolling and rollicking, romping, jumping, bobbing, hopping, springing and swinging and barking and larking about in the snow, Danny Fox, all alone by the tree, crawled into the hole.

He was hungry of course. Except for happy times like the day when the cat stole that cheese for him, he always felt hungry even after meals. The meals were usually small and the five tummies of the family of foxes were large. His tummy was the biggest of the five, but today it had shrunk to nothing, like a burst balloon at the end of a party, because no food had gone into it for a day and a half. He began to crunch the hard-boiled eggs, eating every bit of them including the shells. He forgot that his hind legs and his long bushy tail remained outside the hole.

The wolves were dancing far into the distance, skipping in and out among the trees, but the oldest wolf felt tired. He thought, 'I shall go and talk to the fox until the others come back,' and began to trot slowly towards Danny.

The old wolf was very shortsighted and it happened that the sun shone straight into his eyes. Its rays flickered through the dark evergreen leaves of the fir-trees and made him blink. The snow dazzled him too and to rest his eyes, he tried to look only at the shadows.

These were the shadows of trees, shapely and still, but soon he saw one which moved as though the wind was blowing it. This was the shadow of the tail of Danny Fox which wagged absent-mindedly as he gobbled up the eggs. But the old wolf did not know what it could be. He went up to it cautiously, blinking. Danny heard him from inside the hole and said, 'Hullo' with his mouth full.

'Hullo,' said the wolf to Danny Fox's tail. 'Have you seen a fox anywhere?'

'No. There was a fox here, but he's gone.'

'Then who are you?'

'I am a wolf.'

'Your tail is too bushy and too thick for a wolf and your hind legs are tiny and thin like a rabbit's.'

Danny Fox put on a squeaky voice and said, 'I am a baby wolf.'

'Baby wolves are fluffy and furry. You are shrunken and thin. If you're a wolf at all, you must be a grandfather wolf.'

Danny put on a cracked and trembling voice and said, 'That's right. I'm your grandad.'

'Your tail looks very like a fox's tail,' the old wolf said.

'If you mean that red bushy thing,' said Danny

Fox, 'that's not my tail. That's a broom I was using to sweep the snow away.'

'We'll soon see whether that is true,' the old wolf said, 'I am going to pull you out of that hole and look at your face!'

The old wolf took Danny's tail in his mouth and began to bite and pull.

'Am I hurting you?' he said.

'Oh no,' said Danny. 'That is not my tail you are biting. You've got hold of the broom, can't you see?'

'It's a very hairy broom,' said the wolf.

'That's because it is new.'

'I am still a bit dazzled by the sun,' said the wolf. 'Where's your tail?'

'I'll shake my tail,' said Danny. 'But please don't

bite it.' And he shook the rope which was tied to his neck. The rope was grey.

The old wolf grabbed it and bit it very hard. It broke apart, and Danny pulled the short end into the hole.

'I have broken your tail. Where has it gone?' said the wolf.

Danny Fox pretended to cry, inside the hole. 'You've cut off my tail, you've cut off my beautiful tail!' he cried. But really he was delighted. Now that the rope was broken, he was able to turn round inside the hole. He hid his real tail behind him – his beautiful red, bushy tail with its beautiful white tip – and he put the black tip of his nose outside the hole and saw the six wolves dancing, far, far away.

He was so grateful to the old wolf for setting him free, that he gave him one of the sandwiches. But he did not dare come out of the hole and run away. He knew the old wolf would pounce on him. Instead he barked, and the dancing wolves came racing back to the tree to which they had tied him.

9. Danny is a Prisoner

When the dancing wolves came back, they said, 'Look at the rope! It's broken. Where's the fox?'

'The fox was gone before I got here,' said the oldest wolf, with his mouth full.

'How could he have gone? Who cut the rope?'

'I'm afraid it must have been the grandfather,' said the oldest wolf.

'The grandfather!'

'The grandfather wolf. He is in that hole. I tried to pull him out by the tail but his tail came apart in my mouth.'

'What are you eating? Did you keep some for us? We are hungry!'

'He threw me out a sandwich,' the old wolf said. 'He'll probably give you some.'

'Your grandfather must be very small to be able to get into that hole,' said Danny Fox's special wolf.

'Wolves shrink when they grow old,' the old wolf said.

'Grandad! Grandad!' called the youngest wolf, pushing his face into the hole. 'Give us some sandwiches, Grandad!' The other wolves crowded round him shouting 'Grandad! Grandad! Grandad!' And they all bumped into each other, and growled and snapped and jostled and trod on each other.

The oldest wolf barked at them crossly. 'Stand

back!' he shouted, 'and let me speak to him. Please throw us out some more sandwiches, grandad.'

'None left!' came a muffled voice from the hole.

'None left?' cried the wolves, all together in a rage.

'None!' said the voice. 'But I can give you something else just as good.'

'What can you give us, Grandad?' said the youngest wolf. And the voice answered, 'I'll give you a story to make you forget your hunger!'

'It's Danny Fox!' said the special wolf. 'The cheat! The thief! The villain!'

'I'm not a cheat,' said Danny from inside the hole. 'I am cleverer than you that's all. And the story I am going to tell will show how foxes have always been the cleverest of all creatures since the beginning of the world!'

'I've heard it before,' said the special wolf. But Danny told him he had only heard the first part, and reminded him of how he sneaked away before the end of that.

'Now listen to me, all you wolves,' he said. 'When your brother came to visit me on the other side of the mountain, I told him the story of Reynard the Long-ago Fox, and he didn't feel hungry I am sure. At the beginning of the world, foxes were the only creatures on earth to escape being thrown into the sea. It happened when God created the world and saw that there were no animals in the sea. God told His angel to take a pair of each of the earthly animals and throw them into the sea amongst the fishes. The Angel took one bull and one cow, one sow and one boar, one stag and one hind, one wolf and one she-wolf, and threw them in. And so with all the animals, except the fox who escaped by a trick. The animals soon learned to swim and to stay under water for a long time, and after a year had passed by they did not want to run about on the land any more. They were happy swimming in the sea. All except Reynard the Long-ago Fox who used often to come to the sea-shore and watch them.

'The King of the Sea was a whale, the largest of all the whales, the largest of all the sea animals. And his name was Leviathan. At the end of the year, he called all the sea animals together and counted them.

'"But where is the fox?" said Leviathan when he came to the last pair of animals. And none of them could answer, except two fishes who had watched Reynard tricking the Angel of Death.

'"Please, your Majesty – Oh, great Leviathan!" the fishes said. "The fox is the cleverest of all the animals, on earth or in the sea. He even tricked the Angel of Death. That is why he is not with us."

'Leviathan said, "If he is clever, I must eat his heart. That will make me clever too. Bring Reynard the Fox to me."

'"Oh great Leviathan, we shall bring him to you!" said the first fish.

'"Oh great Leviathan, we shall try to bring him to you!" said the other fish. "But if it is true that he tricked the Angel of Death, how can *we* hope to persuade him to come into the sea?"

'"You must use a cunning argument," Leviathan said.

'"What shall we tell him?"

'"Tell him I am dying," Leviathan said. "Tell him I wish to see him before I die. Tell him I have called all the sea animals together to pay homage to their future king. Tell him that he, King Reynard the Fox, will rule over them as soon as I am dead."

'"All right," said the fishes. "We'll tell him that. Let's go!" And they swam and swam and swam till they reached the seashore.

'Reynard the Fox was playing by the shore as usual, making fountains of sand with his strong paws and picking up pebbles in his mouth and tossing them in the air. And every now and then he would stand still, looking into the sea. When he saw a happy seal, or a dolphin or a porpoise swimming or jumping in and out of the water, he thought to himself "Perhaps it is better to float on the water, than to walk on the land. Those sea animals feel gayer and lighter than I do, perhaps. Perhaps I was wrong not to let the Angel of Death throw me into the sea."

'"Oh, yes, you were wrong," said a watery voice which belonged to one of the fishes.

'"But it's not too late," said another voice, which belonged to the other fish.

'"Who is speaking?" said Reynard the Fox. "I can't see anyone here!" But when he looked into the water he saw two gleaming fish.

'"Who are you?" said Reynard the Fox.

'"We are the King's messengers," they said.

'"But what are your names?"

'"My name is Salmon," said the first fish.

'"And my name is Salmon," said the other one.

'"And what is the name of your King?"

'"His name is Leviathan, King of the Sea."

'"Are you happy?" said Reynard the Fox.

'"We are not happy," said the first salmon. "We are sad because our King Leviathan is dying."

'"Dying?" said Reynard with his head on one side.

'"And we are sad because we have not found the new king," said the other salmon. Then he said, "Who are you?"

'"I am Reynard the Fox."

'"Ah!!' said the salmon, both speaking together. "If you are Reynard the Fox, we have a message for you from the King of the Sea. You must come with us and see him at once."

'"Why?" said Reynard.

'"Our King Leviathan is dying. When we told him that you were the cleverest creature in the world he decided that you should be the next King of the Sea."

'Reynard the Fox wagged his tail, and said, "I was just wondering whether I would be happy in the sea. If I were King of the Sea I know I should be happy."

'"Then come with us quickly. You must see Leviathan before he dies, or he will make some other creature king."

'Reynard the Fox put his toes into the sea and began to shiver. Then a cold white wave broke over him and he swallowed a mouthful of salt water.

'"How can I come with you without drowning?" he said, choking and spluttering and backing away. But the fishes told him he would be quite safe if he rode on their backs.

'"Put two feet on my back," said one.

'"And two on mine," said the other. "And we'll swim on top of the water and you won't even get your toes wet."

'"But Leviathan lives under the water, doesn't he?"

'"He comes up to breathe every quarter of an hour. He will crown you King while you stand on our backs and once you are King of the Sea, the sea will obey you and do you no harm."

'Reynard the Fox believed them, because he was

longing to be king. He stood on their backs and they swam with him far out to sea. At last, he began to feel nervous. When he looked back over his shoulder he saw that the land was out of sight and he said, "I could not turn back now, even if I wished to!"

'The first fish laughed and said, "No, you would drown without us."

'The other fish laughed and said "You will never get back. You are in our power."

'"Be careful. Don't laugh at me. I'll punish you as soon as I am King."

'This made them laugh more. They swam along quickly, laughing all the way, and Reynard did not dare rebuke them for fear they would let him fall into the sea.

'"Why are you laughing?" he asked politely. "Please allow me to share your joke."

'"All right," said the first fish. "We can tell you, now that we know you are too far from land to swim home. You are not going to be King of the Sea."

'"Then Leviathan doesn't want to see me?"

'"Oh, he wants to see you all right."

'"What for?"

'"Because you are clever. He will cut out your heart and eat it, and become as clever as you are."

'"Why didn't you say so at first?" said Reynard the Fox. "Then I'd have brought my heart with me."

'The fishes slowed down and lay still on top of the water, rocking with the waves.

'"Haven't you got your heart with you?" they said.

'"Of course not," said Reynard. "We foxes never carry precious things like hearts about. I keep my heart at home in my den. I only take it out with me when I know I really need it."

'"What shall we do?" said the fishes. "What will Leviathan say?"

'"I don't think he'll say much," said Reynard. "He'll be so cross with you, he'll eat you."

'"What can we do?"

'"Take me back to the land, and I'll fetch my heart. My den is near the shore. It won't take long."

'"No," said the first fish. "We had better see Leviathan first and tell him what has happened. Then go back."

'"You won't have the chance," said Reynard. "He'll be very angry with you."

'"He'll be angrv with you, as well," the second fish said.

'"Oh he won't do me any harm. I'll tell him I offered to fetch my heart, but that you would not take me back."

'"All right, let's go back," said the frightened fish, and they turned round and swam and swam and swam and swam until they reached the sea-shore again. Then Reynard the long-ago Fox leapt off their backs and started jumping about and rolling in the sand.

'"Hurry! Hurry!" called the fishes from the water. "Run and fetch your heart."

'Reynard stopped rolling. He stood up and shook himself and said, "Oh you idiots! If I had not had my heart inside me, how would I have had the heart to ride on your backs out to sea? How would I have had the courage?"

'"You had your heart with you all the time?"

'"Of course. All animals have their hearts with them all the time."

'"You tricked us!"

'"Didn't I trick the Angel of Death himself? You poor little fishes, what made you think you could trick me?"'

Danny Fox was so pleased with his story that he put his head out of the hole and began to show off to the wolves. He tried to come out of the hole altogether, thinking he might jump over their backs and run away, but his tummy was too fat. He had eaten so many sandwiches that he could not get out.

'You think you are like Reynard the Fox,' the oldest wolf said. Danny drew back into the safety of the hole and listened to him. 'You think you have tricked us by pretending to be our grandad and hiding in that little hole where we can't reach you. But now we shall trick you. Come on, wolves, we must dig him out of the earth with our paws and then we shall tie him up again and dance in front of him until he dies.'

10. Danny Fox is Saved

The wolves could not dig Danny out of the hole. They gathered round and scraped the snow away, but the earth beneath it was frozen hard like rock. Even seven wolves with fourteen strong front paws made no impression on it. So Danny Fox was safe. But, he thought to himself, 'I don't want to be safe, if it means staying here in a dark hole on the edge of a strange forest, where no friends ever come. I must see Mrs Doxie Fox again, and Lick and Chew and Swallow. How can I escape from this hole?'

He knew he could not fight the wolves. They were larger than he was. They had longer legs and stronger teeth. The only way to escape from them was by a trick.

'Listen, wolves?' he said. 'I know you want to punish me again.'

They clustered round the hole and peered down at him, sniffing. Seven grey noses filled the entrance to the hole, but none of them could reach him.

'Listen!' he said. 'You may do anything you like with me, but please don't put me out in the snow.'

'Ha-ha!' said the oldest wolf. 'That's just what we shall do.'

'Stand back then,' said Danny. 'Give me plenty of room and I promise to come out and take my punishment.'

'It's a trick. Wait a bit!' said Danny's special wolf. 'If we stand back, he'll run away and we won't be able to catch him.'

And they all came close to the hole again, staring down at Danny.

'I advise you to go away,' said Danny Fox. 'As far away as you can. Because, if you look at the sun, up there in the sky, instead of looking down at me, you will see that it is almost dinner time.'

The oldest wolf looked up at the sky. 'That's true,' he said. 'The sun is half-way up the sky, and that is as far as it goes in winter. This certainly means it is dinner time.'

'The foresters will soon be here,' said Danny. 'They left their dinner in this hole, remember.'

'Do they carry guns?'

'Yes,' said Danny.

'Then I think we'd better move from here. Let's get into the forest and hide among the trees.'

'Be as quick as you can,' said Danny.

'Wait a bit. It's a trick,' said his special wolf. 'He will run away as soon as we've gone.'

'We shall have to take him with us,' said the oldest wolf.

'How can I come with you,' Danny Fox said, 'unless you stand back and let me get out of this hole?' But the special wolf warned them again and they would not stand back.

'Well then,' said Danny. 'I shall stay in here until the foresters have shot you all dead. I think I'll have a little sleep. The sound of their guns will wake me.' He turned round and round, inside the hole, as though he were making a nest, and then lay down and closed his eyes.

Unfortunately he had forgotten about the end of the rope which was still attached to his neck. At first he had been careful to keep it tucked behind him so that no wolf could reach it and pull him out. But when he turned round and round pretending to make a nest to sleep in, he forgot it, and, as he lay down with his eyes closed, its ragged end fell on the earth very

near the entrance to the hole. The oldest wolf saw it at once.

'That is his tail,' he whispered to the others. 'Do you think he is really asleep?'

'That's not his tail,' said the youngest wolf, whispering. 'His tail is red and bushy.'

'It's grey and hard,' the oldest wolf whispered. 'You can't see properly.'

'I can feel, can't I? I bit his tail in two. I know what it's like.'

'Be quiet,' whispered Danny's special wolf. 'Whatever it is, it seems to be attached to him. Why don't we catch hold of it and pull him out?'

'It's the end of the rope,' the youngest wolf said.

'It's the stump of his tail. I bit it. I know it. Watch me while I bite it again.'

Danny Fox heard them whispering but could not make out what they said. He lay still, with his eyes shut, wishing the foresters would come, and he heard no sound as the oldest wolf, crawling flat on his stomach, put his head inside the hole and seized the rope's end in his strong teeth. He pulled.

Danny felt the pull of the knotted rope on his neck and he stuck all four of his feet into the ground and pulled back. With his firm position inside the hole – his hind legs at one side, his forelegs and head at the other – he was able to resist the old wolf for a while, but one by one the other wolves joined in and caught the rope in their teeth and pulled harder and harder, and, as they pulled, the rope drew more and more tightly round Danny Fox's neck until he felt that he would choke.

He tried to hold on to a tree root with his teeth, but the wolves were too strong for him. They growled and pulled and growled and pulled and at last, with one big pull all together, they pulled Danny Fox, choking and spluttering, out into the snow.

Then the oldest wolf let his end of the rope fall into the snow. 'Look how ragged the end of his tail is!' he said.

The youngest wolf let go of the rope and shouted angrily, 'That's not his tail. That is the rope. His tail is bushy and red.'

'It's ragged and grey,' said the oldest wolf.

'It's bushy and red!'

'It's grey!'

'It's red!'

'It's grey!'

'Oh, you silly old fool!' said the youngest wolf. 'Can't you see he'll escape if you argue with me like this?'

The youngest wolf caught hold of the rope again, but the oldest wolf went prowling round in a huff.

Then he said to Danny Fox 'What colour is your tail?'

'Grey,' said Danny. 'It looks very like a rope.'

'Do you hear that?' said the oldest wolf, coming close to the youngest and growling.

'I'll show it to you,' said the youngest wolf. He tried to grab hold of Danny's bushy red tail, but Danny turned quickly to face him. They snarled at each other.

'What colour is your tail? Tell the truth or I'll bite you.'

'Grey,' said Danny, 'and as smooth as a rope!'

The young wolf jumped over Danny and pounced on his bushy red tail, gripping it firmly in his huge jaws. Danny twisted his head back and caught him by the leg and they rolled over and over, growling and snarling, in the snow. The other wolves, who had been holding the rope all this time, let go when they saw a fight had begun and jumped on top of Danny and the youngest wolf. And now there was a struggling, snapping, snarling heap of wolves all trying to bite Danny Fox. He heard their angry growling and heavy snorting breath, as they tried to get at him with their teeth, and he knew that with seven large wolves against him, he could not win a fight. But the nearest one to him was the old wolf and he managed to whisper in his ear, 'Would you like to see my grey tail once more?'

'Yes, of course.'

'I'll put it into your mouth,' said Danny. 'But please don't bite it hard.'

The old wolf said nothing but he had made up his mind to bite it as hard as he could. Danny twisted and turned underneath the heap of wolves until he was able to catch hold of the youngest wolf's tail.

'Here it is,' he said to the old one. 'Now is it grey or red?'

'I'm so close I can see it clearly now,' said the oldest wolf. 'It is grey, all right.' And he gave it a tremendous bite.

The youngest wolf yelped and turned on him at once, and they began to fight each other furiously and as they fought they grew blind with rage and forgot why they were fighting and began to bite their friends, and their friends, not knowing who had bitten them, bit the nearest wolf in revenge until all seven wolves were fighting with each other, in a large, grey, heaving, snarling, yelping heap. Danny Fox was underneath them all, lying flat in the snow unable to move. He was very much afraid that soon they might stop fighting and remember him. The wolves tugged and pulled at each other with their hard teeth, and rage made them deaf. They did not hear the crunch of the foresters' boots in the snow. The first thing they heard was the gun.

BANG! went the gun and a bullet whizzed over them. They stopped fighting at once and crouched down for five seconds, not knowing which way to run, and now Danny Fox was glad they were on top of him, shielding him from the bullets. He could not see out between their legs and did not know that the foresters were hiding behind trees, afraid to show themselves to seven hungry wolves. There were three foresters. They had only one gun between them. It was old and could only shoot one bullet at a time.

The foresters loaded their gun again and fired. BANG went the gun and this time the bullet whizzed past the oldest wolf's nose, but just missed him. He snapped at it, and growled, not knowing

what it was, then jumped across the other wolves and ran into the forest. They followed him quickly and very soon they were all out of sight.

Danny Fox looked up and saw no wolves. He saw no foresters either because they had run into the forest after the wolves. When he saw that all was safe, he crept quietly away from the trees, walking painfully along by the bottom of the cliff. One of the wolves had bitten his foot and wherever he walked he left red specks of blood on the snow. He looked up at the cliff from time to time and thought how easy it was to come down it, higgledy-piggledy, tied to the wolf in the blinding snow, but how impossible to climb it.

He walked on and on, hoping to find a gently sloping place where he might climb the cliff. He was afraid the foresters would come after him following his trail, and he hurried as much as he could, but the snow was deep and heavy to walk in. He was lame in one leg where the wolf had bitten him, and he could not run.

The cliff above him seemed higher and steeper at every step, and at the end of the afternoon, when the sun went down, he was so tired that he lost hope of ever reaching home. He sat down in the snow and licked his sore paw. It was almost dark by now, but the snowy ground reflected the sky with a ghostly light.

It was lucky for Danny that the light was ghostly and hard to see by, for the foresters, as soon as they had lost track of the wolves, had come back to the place where they had hidden their sandwiches. When they saw how their dinner had been stolen, they shrugged their shoulders and were ready to go back to work again, but then they saw Danny's footsteps and the specks of blood. They forgot all about their work, and spent the whole afternoon tracking him down, until at sunset they saw him licking his paw beneath the cliff.

The forester who carried the gun held up his hand to keep the others quiet. They crouched behind him as he knelt in the snow and fired at Danny. He fired – BANG – but the light was bad and he missed. Danny Fox jumped up, yelping with surprise, and began to hobble and hop away, half-running on his lame leg. The foresters came after him, but they could hardly see him and suddenly they stopped to listen. They heard his yelps, but now the yelps seemed to come from the top of the cliff above them. They looked up and saw the head of a small fox, who was leaning over the edge of the cliff.

Danny Fox heard the yelping too. He looked up and saw Swallow. There was a bang as the foresters shot at Swallow (but again they missed) and Swallow, on top of the cliff, ran yelping at Danny below – 'This way, this way!'

Danny Fox ran limping along by the foot of the cliff underneath him. He thought the foresters would follow him, but they had seen two other foxes on top of the cliff and these foxes ran in the opposite direction. The foresters shot at them, but missed again in the bad light, and turned back to follow them away from Danny Fox. These two other foxes were Lick and Chew. By showing themselves to the foresters they gave Swallow time to lead Danny to a gap in the cliff.

'Here it is,' said Swallow to Danny. 'We discovered it together, Lick, Chew and me and if we hadn't seen you from the top, we were going to climb down and search for you in the strange country. Oh dear – you've hurt your paw!'

Danny Fox had climbed up through the steep gap in the cliff, following the bed of a stream.

'Have you been searching for me?'

'Yes. Since last night when you didn't come home. Lick and Chew thought the ram had killed you. They said the wolf was right to be afraid of sheep.'

'Well,' said Danny. 'Perhaps the ram did nearly kill me, because if it had not been for him, I would not have had to fight the seven wolves.'

Swallow licked his father's paw, and Danny began to feel better. Then his other children came – Lick and Chew, barking and boasting about their chase with the foresters.

'Come on!' they said. 'Those men have gone home. We'd better go home too.'

'Can you remember the way?' said Lick.

'Can you remember the way?' said Chew.

'I can't,' said Danny. 'I was pulled here by the wolf.'

But Swallow said, 'I can remember the way.

Follow me!' He set off across the snowy plain, and the others followed in single file.

The snow became thin and the breeze warmer, and at last they left the snowy land. They walked on green grass, and began to climb a hill. They walked on little stones and began to climb the mountain. They walked on rocks and were near the big pond. They walked round the pond and climbed the flat rock. And then, one after another, they jumped off the rock and ran down the mountain path towards their den. Even Danny Fox ran, with his lame leg, and they all arrived together like one excited bundle of red fur and fell together, tumbling over one another, into their den, near Mrs Doxie Fox's feet.

'Oh Danny,' she said, 'I am glad you are safe!' and he told her how Lick, Chew and Swallow had found him. 'They must be hungry,' he said.

'Well, children,' said Mrs Doxie Fox. 'I have a large pile of bones here, which the farmer's wife threw out. Would you like to eat those, or would you prefer a good story?'

They knew she was joking and all answered, 'Bones!' When they had eaten them and were lying down to sleep, Danny found that he could stretch out his legs without touching the others.

'The den seems bigger,' he said.

'I made it bigger,' said Swallow.

'He found a soft place in the wall,' said Lick.

'Near the floor,' said Chew. 'And we dug.'

'I am glad,' said Danny. 'You have all grown so big. We needed more room.'

'Oh, I didn't do it for us,' said Swallow. 'It was to make room for the wolf *and us*, next time he comes to stay.'

Some other Young Puffins

PUGWASH AND THE MUTINY and PUGWASH AND THE FANCY-DRESS PARTY

John Ryan

Another pair of amazing adventures of the much-loved Captain Pugwash in which he is rescued from tricky situations by cabin-boy Tom.

THE CONKER AS HARD AS A DIAMOND

Chris Powling

A lively title for a really lively book! Little Alpesh's burning ambition is to find a diamond-hard conker to make him champion of the universe. A zany story, sparkling with fun, to delight conker fiends.

ELOISE

Kay Thompson

At the Plaza Hotel, surrounded by her dog, her turtle, her nanny and a host of hotel guests, six-year-old Eloise is never bored . . .

RETURN TO OZ

L. Frank Baum and *Alistair Hedley*

Dorothy knows that her friends and the Emerald City must be saved from the evil Nome King, the cruel Princess Mombi and the terrifying squealing Wheelers. So, with some strange companions, Tik-Tok, Jack Pumpkinhead and a talking hen, Billina, she sets off on a frightening, mysterious and exciting adventure.

THE TALE OF GREYFRIARS BOBBY

Lavinia Derwent

A specially retold version for younger readers of the true story of a little Skye terrier who was faithful to his master even in death.

LITTLE DOG LOST

Nina Warner Hooke

The adventures of Pepito, a scruffy black and white puppy who lives in an old soap powder box in Spain. The excitement starts when the rubbish collectors sweep Pepito up in his box and deposit him at the bottom of a disused quarry, miles from anywhere!

SATURDAY BY SEVEN
Penelope Farmer

Peter should have been saving for a month to get the money needed to go camping with the Cubs. Now there is only one day left, and how can he possibly earn it in time?

THE WORST WITCH
Jill Murphy

Mildred Hubble had a reputation for being the worst pupil in Miss Cackle's school for witches. So when things started to go wrong at the Hallowe'en celebrations, she was naturally at the centre of it all.

TWO VILLAGE DINOSAURS
Phyllis Arkle

Two dinosaurs spell double trouble as Dino and Sauro trample their amiable way through the village, causing chaos and confusion on every side!

BRINSLY'S DREAM
Petronella Breinburg

'Never be afraid. You're as good as the next man,' Brinsly told himself, and he threw himself heart and soul into getting his football team up to scratch for the big match.

STORIES FOR UNDER-FIVES
MORE STORIES FOR UNDER-FIVES
STORIES FOR FIVE-YEAR-OLDS
STORIES FOR SIX-YEAR-OLDS
STORIES FOR SEVEN-YEAR-OLDS
MORE STORIES FOR SEVEN-YEAR-OLDS
STORIES FOR EIGHT-YEAR-OLDS
STORIES FOR NINE-YEAR-OLDS
STORIES FOR TENS AND OVER
edited by Sara and Stephen Corrin

Celebrated anthologies of stories especially selected for each age group and tested in the classroom by the editors.

KATY AND THE NURGLA
Harry Secombe

Katy had the whole beach to herself, until an old, tired monster swam up to the very rock where she was sitting reading. Harry Secombe's first book for children has all the best ingredients in just the right proportions: a monster, a spaceship, adventure, humour and more than a touch of happy sadness.

DORRIE AND THE BIRTHDAY BOOK
Patricia Coombs

When the eggs for the Big Witch's birthday cake get broken by mistake, Dorrie sets off to buy some more from the Egg Witch. But her errand takes her through the forest, and lurking there is Thinnever Vetch, all ready to make mischief . . .

DINNER AT ALBERTA'S

Russell Hobdan

Arthur the crocodile has extremely bad table manners until he is invited to dinner at Alberta's.

MRS PEPPERPOT'S YEAR

Alf Prøysen

'Goodness,' said the little girl in hospital when she saw that the nice old lady who was tucking her in had suddenly shrunk to a few inches high, 'you must be Mrs Pepperpot!'
'Right first time,' said Mrs Pepperpot, 'and now it's your turn to help me.'

CARROT TOPS

John Wyatt

Fifteen stories of everyday events like making a jelly, growing a carrot-top garden, visiting Granny – all tinged with the make-believe that young children love.

ONE NIL

Tony Bradman

Dave Brown is mad about football, and when he learns that the England squad are to train at the local City ground he thinks up a brilliant plan to overcome his parents' objections and get him to the ground to see them.

ON THE NIGHT WATCH

Hannah Cole

A group of children and their parents occupy their tiny school in an effort to prevent its closure.

FIONA FINDS HER TONGUE

Diana Hendry

At home Fiona is a chatterbox, but whenever she goes out she just won't say a word. How she overcomes her shyness and 'finds her tongue' is told in this charming book.

IT'S TOO FRIGHTENING FOR ME!

Shirley Hughes

The eerie old house gives Jim and Arthur the creeps. But somehow they just can't resist poking around it, even when a mysterious white face appears at the window! A deliciously scary story – for brave readers only!

THE GHOST AT NO. 13

Gyles Brandreth

Hamlet Brown's sister, Susan, is just too perfect. Everything she does is praised and Hamlet is in despair – until a ghost comes to stay for a holiday and helps him to find an exciting idea for his school project!

RADIO DETECTIVE

John Escott

A piece of amazing deduction by the Roundbay Radio Detective when Donald, the radio's young presenter, solves a mystery but finds out more than anyone expects.

RAGDOLLY ANNA'S CIRCUS

Jean Kenward

Made only from a morsel of this and a tatter of that, Ragdolly Anna is a very special doll, and the six stories in this book are all about her adventures.

SEE YOU AT THE MATCH

Margaret Joy

Six delightful stories about football. Whether spectator, player, winner or loser, these short, easy stories for young readers are a must for all football fans.